Sixty Days

Sixty Days

Hernan Jaen

I dedicate this book to my wife, my son, my parents as well as a very special person, a real friend, who believed in me and in my first project, Miguel Ángel De Gracia Chávez (r.i.p.)

Table of Contents

           Extradition Case· 104
Chapter 22 The Narcotics Agreements for Extradition Issues· · · · · 110
Chapter 23 New Changes · 113
Chapter 24 The Contact with the Judges · · · · · · · · · · · · · · · · · · 119
Chapter 25 One Year Later · 122
Chapter 26 I Have No Answers From My Lawyer · · · · · · · · · · · · · 124
Chapter 27 One Year and Eleven Months After the Arrest · · · · · · · 128

           About the Author · 137
           Bibliography· 139

SIXTY DAYS–A BOOK BASED ON A TRUE STORY

A BUSINESS TRIP BECOMES HIS WORST NIGHTMARE

For a successful forty-four year old businessman, a business trip turns out to be the worst experience of his life. Everything got more complicated when, among the people he met during the first two days after his arrival, nobody spoke English.

However, he has to fight for the truth and for his dignity at all costs. Fortunately, he creates a strong bond with a young lawyer who believes in him and decides to support him with all his soul.

This international story tells about a social topic and a crime that the United States has been fighting against in recent years, and one of the largest operations in the history of INTERPOL. This operation has been reported in the New York Times and in the most prestigious newspapers in the United States, India and Central America.

The story is based on a real life legal issue that involves three countries. If the characters' real names were revealed, a lot of information about this story could be confirmed on the internet.

Having a book based on real events in the category of bestsellers is important, but the fact of telling this story to the world and that many people can benefit from it is not only interesting, but also rewarding.

Exciting moments of adventure and action combined with mystery and suspense make it a book suitable to any type of audience.

I do not consider it a book for self-motivation and improvement, but since it is based on a real- life situation; it could fall into this category, considering it deals with life issues such as endurance and self-determination through a different and spectacular international story whose main character gets free from the clutches of injustice after a strong battle.

CHAPTER 1

A Desperate Call

Panama, Panama City. July 18th, 2015

WHILE I WAS DRIVING THE car, I synchronized the mobile phone so I could call my wife. By that time, I was already a married man who enjoyed keeping in touch with his wife and his one-year-old baby boy.

I asked her the usual question in a humorous and cheerful tone:

"Hello, sugar! How are you doing it? And how is my little boy?"

"Well, honey, I am here with him."(She took a picture and sent it to me.)

When I saw the picture, I felt that father's pride blended with tenderness and hope.

While we were both enjoying our little son, I got a call from the office. I didn't know that call would be the start of the best and most fascinating story of my life, something I would never forget.

"Regina, baby, a call from the office is coming in. I will call you later."

"Ok, baby, "she replied.

I answered the phone and Sara, the secretary, said: "Hello, Henry, a man from India just called us telling about a detainee in Panama; in five minutes, he will call you.

"This gentleman seems too desperate," added the secretary.

A few minutes later, my cell phone rang. I heard a very agitated and trembling voice. He spoke English with an accent.

"Siiiiiiiiirrrrrrrrrr Siiiiiiiiirrrrrrrrrrr, we need help. Please, Mr. Lawyer."

When you hear a voice like that, you know something is wrong. In fact, there are calls that change your perception about important life issues. This was one of those, when you realized that a person and a whole family's life are being destroyed.

"Yes, tell me, how can I help you?" I peacefully replied, trying to minimize his obvious despair.

"My name is Amil and I'm from India. My best friend is detained in Panama.

"Calm down, please...Tell me...Why has he been detained?"

"We do not know the reasons; we believe it is the United States government."

And he started begging, "I need you to go to see him now, please."

I asked him another important question:

"When was your friend detained in Panama?"

Amil answered: "On July, 15th"

It had been two days before. I knew where he was. After two days of detention, prisoners are taken from the prosecutor's office detention center at the airport to the preventive detention, which is a kind of human deposit where all the detainees go.

An Unfriendly Small Place.

I was in trouble because, since I didn't expect to attend any customers, I was not wearing the formal outfit. Besides, in my country, most lawyers wear casual clothes to work on Fridays. However, because of the urgency of the case, I committed to do it even though I was uncomfortable with not following the dressing code. I was wearing a long-sleeved shirt, but it is not enough if you are visiting a detainee for the first time.

I had to act as fast as possible. Going back home to change my clothes would have represented not only a waste of time, but also the possibility to lose the case since the customer's emergency would have led him to look for another lawyer, which is perfectly understandable.

I arrived at about 2:00 p.m. The call had been made twenty minutes before. When I entered, I asked for Mr. Ritesh Ambani. At that moment, I saw a man of 1.65 meters tall, with Indian features. I knew right away he had to be the one I was looking for. It was unnecessary to talk to him by the phone behind the glass because by chance he was being taken to court at the time I arrived.

We were seeing each other face to face when I asked: "Are you, Ritesh Ambani?"

He nodded while saying: "Yes, I am Ritesh, I am Ritesh!!" My presence without a doubt excited him.

I introduced myself and said, "Hi, Ritesh! My name is Henry Lopez. We received a call from Amil, one of your friends in India and that's why I'm here."

He gave me some copies and said: "This is my case. Read it, please. Today in the morning, two lawyers came. These are the lawyers." He showed me one lawyer's card, which discouraged me a little bit. This card represented one of the largest law firms in Panama. That law firm alone had an army of lawyers. I knew it was difficult to compete with them, so while they were taking him in handcuffs to court, I told him: "Well, if you already have a lawyer, then I'm leaving."

He looked back and said out loud while he was being taken to a patrol car: "Henry, if you are with Amil, I am with you." Then, a policeman put his head down and forced him into the car.

When I arrived at the preventive, I realized that Ambani already had an appeal to the court. Everything had happened so fast! They had called us a little late, but when there is a will, there is a way. I ran to my car and headed towards the court, trying to reach the patrol where Ambani had left.

CHAPTER 2

My First Job

Panama, Panama City, 2005
Ten years before

I WAS TWENTY-TWO YEARS OLD when I met the woman who is nowadays my wife. We were both studying at the university. At that age, she became my girlfriend. As every young man having a lovely relationship, I knew it implied going to the movies, going out to eat, giving details to the person. As a result, I needed to have my money, so I started looking for a job.

The university where I studied had a morning and an evening shift to meet the individual needs of each student. If I wanted to work, I had to enroll in the evening shift, so I did it.

As a law student, I could choose a job as an intern or paralegal, but when checking online on the job boards, there were few of them. I got information about a job that had nothing to do with my career, but it had more advertisements (ads) and the payment was similar.

THE AD SAID:
Call Center looks for sellers online.
Requirements: Excellent English
Experience in other call centers.
Send your resume to this email address: _____

And so I did... I sent my resume.

Three days later, I went to an interview. I attended it without knowing that some years later, I would understand the great impact that such a simple job would have in my life due to the valuable knowledge I got from it.

When I arrived, I felt fascinated by the building. It was a new and spectacular 21-story building. The office was on the top floor, 400 meters high, where there were three more offices.

The whole atmosphere delighted me from the first time I saw it. "Someday, when I become a lawyer, I will open my office in this building", I told myself. Experience has shown that when we strive to achieve our dreams, they come true. Some people called it "The law of attraction", others call if "Faith". Years later, I had my office in that same building

When I arrived at the office, I rang the doorbell and the receptionist answered. I told her my name and the reason for my visit. She made a call and, a few minutes later, I could get in.

When I entered, I found different cubicles. There were around thirty-five or forty young people sitting at their desks with a pair of headphones. Most of them were as young as I, but there were also some older ones. I walked through the call center until I got to the final office where the owner was supposed to interview me.

INTRODUCING HIMSELF:

"Good Morning! How are you?" "My name is Roberto Alvarado, one of the company's associates. We are three owners: Two Panamanians and an American."

I introduced myself: "My name is Henry Lopez, and it is a great pleasure. I come for the internet announcement."

"Yeah, sure! Take a seat," He replied.

He spoke in both languages to test my English mastery.

Tell me… "How do you see this place? He asked.

"Very nice, I like it a lot," I answered enthusiastically.

"Tell me about you, I want to hear you speak English. Show me what you have. We'll see if it's true."

For English, there was no problem. Even though I speak it with an accent, it is understandable and communicative, so I talked to him in English.

"Well… My name is Henry Lopez. I'm interested in working in a call center during the daytime since I study at night."

At that moment, Roberto asked: "And what do you study, Henry?"

"Law", I replied.

"Oh! A lawyer in the Call Center! Ha! Ha! Ha! How nice it is to have a lawyer to defend us if we get into a serious problem!" Hahaha!!

But, he told me later: "It's a joke, Henry, what problem are we going to get ourselves into? No, no way!"

All of a sudden, his laughter turned into a serious look, and by staring at me, he asked: "Henry, have you ever worked in a Call Center? Look, that's the main thing I'm looking for."

And I replied: "To be honest, no. But, if you give me the opportunity, I can gain experience."

He lowered his face and said: "Look, Henry, everyone you see here comes from other call centers."

I looked at them; they were all busy talking to their clients.

My interviewer's face seemed familiar. I knew that I had seen him before or met him from another place; Then, I remembered we had studied at the same school, but he was several years older than I. He was four levels ahead. I saw my lack of experience as a difficult issue at that moment, so it was time to use our familiarity as a strategy.

Then, I said: "I believe that we studied at the same school, I am the son of the teacher …."

And he answered immediately: Oh, my teacher!

To be honest, if I had not said that, maybe they would have never hired me.

Then, he continued: "You have two things that I like a lot. First, you have a good mastery of English. Second, you are a clever young man. Come tomorrow! There will be a 15-day training to explain how everything works. You will understand the whole business and will develop selling strategies. There is a whole group that will be taking the training."

He stood up, and while extending his hand to shake mine, he said: "It's a pleasure, Henry. Thanks for coming; I'll wait for you tomorrow at 9:00 a.m."

I turned, walked away through the Call Center and left.

The next day, I went to the training given by the Call Center Manager. She had worked in three call centers

and had all the experience required. Indeed, she was like a Magister in Call Centers.

There were ten young people in the training. Most of them were my age but a few looked older.

The manager introduced herself:

"Good morning, young people. My name is Claudia, I am the company's manager and today we begin what will be a fifteen-day training, which will be remunerated. I will begin by explaining what the company is about. It is an online pharmacy whose most clients are from the United States.

I raised my hand and signaled to the trainer to let her know that I was not a pharmacist.

She told me, "Do not worry. From now on, we will teach you a lot about this business."

That online pharmacy would provide valuable knowledge in my life that would be very useful later. I researched and learned so much that I became an empirical pharmacist.

Roberto entered with his partner; the other Panamanian named Octavio and introduced him to the ten boys there. When I finished the training, I had already learned what I needed to start with and I was ready to join the team, which in total turned out to be composed of fifty members, including my group.

THE FIRST DAY OF WORK.

I was adjusting the headphones when I felt Roberto's and Octavius's eyes from the distance. Both seemed to be talking about me, but I did not pay too much attention. Instead, I continued working.

Roberto felt happy because the business was growing. I heard a conversation between them.

Roberto: "We already have the ten new boys. The team is growing, Octavio. Look, they all have Call Center experience except for the one named Henry."

Octavio, feeling surprised, asked: "And why did you hire him if he has no experience"

"I analyzed the situation," Roberto told him. "He speaks English and comes from the same prestigious school where I graduated. Besides, he is clever and fast at answering questions."

Roberto was a twenty-nine-year-old man who had already built his own company, which was in continuous growth. At that moment, He had over thirty employees.

Octavio shook his head in denial and said: "We had agreed that everyone had to have experience. Put him the one- week test. If he does not sell the minimum per week, he has to leave."

Roberto looked down and showed agreement by saying a simple, but not too convincing "Ok."

In the call center, I felt like a fish in the water. Indeed, I fell in love with selling. I focused my mind on the fact that being a salesperson is challenging but fun. For every sale I made, I had to get up and write it on a front panel which also had the number of sales made by each employee monthly. I did not want to be left behind.

When the first month was over, Roberto stood in front of everyone and pointed out that he had something to say. It was a general meeting for the whole team and he started by saying: "Hello guys, I want to take a break today to talk to you about something important. Here I have the numbers of all of you, the daily sales. There are several that keep them low."

I realized that some of them had not even written. There was a girl who had not sold a single medication in the whole month. She was so frustrated that she felt her end was near. But others were very competent and used to sell all the medicines.

Roberto proceeded: "Young people, there is a person in the group whose numbers I will mention. Unlike you, this boy has no experience in call centers. However, he has exceeded my expectations. He showed my sales on the board with great enthusiasm.

Day of the Week	Number of Sales
Monday	7
Tuesday	11
Wednesday	9
Thursday	8
Friday	8

He continued his lecture: "Today is Friday, there are still some hours left. He has sold 43 medications so far this week. I am really surprised by his results! Not only has he passed the test, but he is among my five best sellers.

He made a pause… Then, after a big breath, he said: "If he could do it having no previous experience, what is wrong with you guys?"

I felt like a superhero that day. These things made me happy and motivated me to keep moving.

I knew I could not drop my numbers if I wanted to continue. That day, I received my second check and deposited it in a bank account I had opened recently.

I loved the place. There was a good atmosphere. Basically, the business was that they provided us with lists of people's names that were automatically placed on the computer. We had to call them to their numbers to sell them drugs. These customers appeared on the list because they had already made purchases.

I learned and increased my knowledge a lot because I researched about the drugs, their functions, and their components. Besides, I was lucky to have a companion over 40 years old beside me who also dispelled my doubts because of the vast experience she got by working on this in the United States.

BRENDA'S LEGACY

"Brenda, why do customers buy so much Hydrocodone? It's the most sold medicine here."

To which Brenda responded: "Because that is a narcotic people become addicted to. It is a pain medication, but it is addictive. If you look at the lists, you will see the names of people for whom it has been prohibited and therefore their names appear in red."

It was a shame that these addicted people, who appeared in red in the lists, asked for more and more, willing to spend all their money on that. With Brenda by my side, I learned a lot about medications. Narcotic analgesics like Hydrocodone and non- narcotic analgesics such as Tramadol. When I was younger, I learned everything fast. Besides, I had become an expert in medicines of all kinds because, unlike some of my colleagues, I liked to research and go further. I was interested in asking and learning more every day. I sold all kinds of medications and when there was something I didn't know, I would either ask Brenda or investigate it by myself.

BRENDA'S REMARKS

Brenda once told me, "I can see that you analyze a little bit more than the rest, I do not know if it's because of your career, but you ask and go further and see life from another point of view. These other young people, even though they are the same age, they do not know what they are doing. They are like robots making calls."

I had learned so much about medicines that I considered myself a pharmacist. I knew a lot about them, their components, the different laboratories they were made at, etc.

But eventually, I realized that I had to stop because I also needed to focus on my law career. So, I gave up what had been a beautiful and interesting experience. I stopped working and focused on my studies.

Living under my parents' roof, there was a rule set by my mother and it was that I had to work or study, either of the two options, but I could not stay in the house doing anything. When I was in college, she did not have any complaint. So, I stayed at home trying to fulfill my university duties.

CHAPTER 3

Gaining Experience

Three years later
Panama City, 2008

By the year 2008, a few months after my wife and I graduated, we started looking for a job. Experience is fundamental and it was necessary to gain it to start at a large law firm, which was our aim.

I went to a job interview which made me feel excited. When I spoke on the phone, I felt the voice of an older person. He said: "Look, come to my house and I'll explain what it is about." He gave me the address.

Upon arriving, I saw that it was a building in a luxurious area of Panama. I announced in the booth and then I called from the intercom. A man opened the door and I went up to his apartment.

When I arrived, I could see that it was a huge apartment, a penthouse, in fact. The man was an elderly American gentleman who, with a friendly voice, invited me to sit down.

I sat down and made myself comfortable while he settled in a kind of office in the middle of the room, where he kept writing on the computer. Then, he got up and stood in front of me in the living room.

He told me: "You are young, how old are you"?

"I'm 25 years old," I answered.

He told me his name and pointed from the window and in the distance to another large commercial building. "Do you see that building over there?" He asked---"There I have my offices; I have 5 Panamanian lawyers working for me"

I already knew that he had his offices in that building because I had investigated it.

"My business is to make offshore corporations and sell these companies around the world", He told me, "Look, the reason for calling you is because I need a bank that opens accounts without customers having to come to Panama. If I can find one, I can do a lot of business with international clients."

I said, "Well, I've heard something about it, but I have to investigate more."

We sat down to talk and the gentleman told me one by one the whole structure of his business. I do not know if because of my young age, but I perceived that he underestimated me.

At the University, I had learned to make corporations, but no teacher spoke to us with so much knowledge about this topic. The professors from the university in charge of teaching us about commercial law were short compared to this gentleman in the subject of offshore companies. This gentleman was a teacher and a businessman, a real expertise.

That day, I listened with great attention and kept in my memory every detail.

I remember that before leaving, he accompanied me to the door and I asked him the following question:

"Are you a lawyer?"

"No, I'm a businessman, he replied.

This man, without being a lawyer, had become a millionaire in a business intended for national citizens. For me, this man had a superior mind. Thanks to him, I got very important knowledge that I have kept as a secret and valued as a treasure. He was a fundamental part of my story because what I learned from him changed my life forever.

Years later, he had a problem with one of his lawyers for an economic issue. The lawyer sued him, so he had to close his business.

PANAMA, PANAMA CITY, 2009.

By the year 2009, we had set up our own office. I had everything struc-
tured as I learned it from the master, the American gentleman. This
was a good year for offshore companies. Large firms had control and
monopoly, and thousands of offshore companies were created per year.
We did not create millions of companies, but we did many. Every day,
people from all over the world called us to buy corporations.

Several law firms that were twenty and thirty years old had become
millionaires with these offshore corporations. What happened with
Panama Papers is true; we were witnesses of that by being into the
game just for a few months. However, the success of the offshore companies was not for us because when we entered the business, the government had other plans with them. We had to continue with other areas
of law.

We could not enjoy for a long time because by the year 2010, the
government had signed agreements to exchange financial information,
taking Panama out of the list of tax havens. To a great extent, from my
point of view, this affected the country and all the lawyers. The econ-
omy and the big banks in Panama do not depend only on The Panama
Canal and tourism, but also on big companies that keep their money in
Panama, some of them to evade taxes.

The year 2010 was a very tough one for offshore companies, but The
Panama Papers incident in 2016 ended up destroying them. I remember that call during the first months of 2016, from a person who asked
us about offshore companies. He spoke English as a Native American
speaker.

In the end, he asked me: "Have you heard about the anonymous
group?"

I said, "I used to enter your page when I did not want to be tracked
by another page"

Then, he replied with a sarcastic tone: "We're not all bad."

The day after his call, I received a cell phone message from a cousin
early in the morning asking "Are you watching the news? Look at what

happened to that Panamanian Law Firm". I turned on the TV and it was in all the national and international media.

This coincided with what the owner of the firm said that they had been hacked. I did not know if by accident, but that happened to us. Nevertheless, I read no news that pointed to this anonymous group as responsible for what happened.

CHAPTER 4

Control Audience Or
Presentation Hearing

Upon arriving at the Court, I saw that Mr.Ambani was sitting on the bench of the accused, the three judges were in their places and the prosecutor was representing the Public Prosecutor of Panama. Ritesh was handcuffed and with shackles on his feet, and next to him, there was a translator or interpreter from the Government.

The three judges were explaining about his detention and the process he would have to go through in Panama. I could see other lawyers in the defense of Ambani. I had not arrived before because they had called me a little bit late, but this is how it is. It is mandatory to act fast. Otherwise, another one takes your place.

I realized that the card that Ambani had shown me did not belong to a big law firm. The large law firm was sitting next to the Public Prosecutor's Office, representing the United States government; those who represented Ambani belong to a small firm.

At that moment, I received messages from Amil's WhatsApp, Ritesh's friend from India, and I explained to him that Ritesh was already being defended by other lawyers and that they were already sitting taking their place of representation. Very discreetly, I took a picture for his family to see him.

Amil told me: "Do not abandon Ritesh, please. I want you to join the other lawyers; I want you all to defend him."

To be honest, I always prepare myself for each case. When I have a criminal case, I take it with a lot of responsibility. Sometimes, I do not even sleep at night when working on them. But the criminal cases that I had attended were all minimal compared to this.

Extradition cases are different. I even know famous lawyers among the best criminal lawyers in the country who have never seen a single case of extradition. Extradition cases are more international and more complex. If we compare it with the medical field, it would be like dealing with brain surgeries or heart transplants. To this; add the press, the national and international media.

Sometimes the country requesting the detainee is a powerful one and the pressure they exert is enormous. In our country, as in many countries, there is no specialization in extradition cases; extradition is a part of Private International Law. Most of the specialists in this field have never seen a case of extradition in court because extradition cases are few.

The extradition cases in Panama have been attended by the country's largest criminal lawyers and have handled high-profile national cases. I consider the lawyer, who had the most extradition cases, an extradition specialist.

I was sitting in the audience, and in the position of Ritesh's lawyers, there were two, taking the place and not willing to give that position to anyone. The three judges explained the reason for the hearing, and they clarified to Mr.Ambani the reason he was being detained for. They argued that he would be taken to an extradition process in Panama at the request of the United States' government. The Public Ministry had appointed a translator who would be at his side at all times so that he could understand the hearing.

Once the hearing opened, the Prosecutor was given the opportunity to begin his defense:

"Good afternoon, gentlemen and judges, defense party, general audience."

"My name is Yolanda Rivera and I am the Prosecutor in the Public's representation Ministry. We have received through the Foreign Ministry the request for Extradition of Mr. Ritesh Ambani, for the following charges:

1. Conspiracy to import non-narcotic drug category IV.
2. Money Laundering through an online pharmacy owned by Mr. Ritesh Ambani, which he operates to sell these types of medicines that have no prescription and may be forged. The four medications in question are Tramadol, Carisoprodol, Viagra, and Cialis."

She continued reading a two-long page brief within Ritesh's file. Since I had worked in the Call Center, I knew these four medicines.

Once the Prosecutor finished, the judge presiding the hearing addressed the Prosecutor and thanked her for her participation, then talked with the lawyers and told them that it was their turn to exercise the defense.

One lawyer representing Ritesh talked and had his chance to express what he considered.

A veteran lawyer who was attending the hearing, and was sitting behind me, but who had nothing to do with the case entered as a mere spectator since anyone can witness this type of audience. Although the room was not full, there were other lawyers, interns, and a few law students among the public.

The veteran lawyer told me: "There must be a lot of money here"

I asked him several questions in a row: "And how do you know? Why do you say it? Do you know the detainee? Were you also called to the case?"

The veteran lawyer answered: "No, I came to see other cases that I have in this court, and this one had caught my attention because it is a case of extradition, so I stayed here for a while to witness it. Not every day you see something like this, son."

"This is a serious case; these two lawyers have to be charging a lot of money."

In my mind, I said to myself: "If you knew that I was called to this too."

His white mustache and his look reflected many years of experience and, to be honest, he did not look like a lawyer, but as a judge because of his mature age. Then, I dared to say: "You know what….I was also called for this case, but they called me late."

The veteran lawyer answered: "In the recess when the judges leave, get up and talk to the judge's secretary and explain the situation, and also to the Prosecutor. If you were called for this, you must let them know you are also part of the case."

Following his advice, I approached the prosecutor, but she responded with pure denials. All she said was "no". She made emphasis on the fact that the other lawyers had already introduced themselves as the ones in charge of the case. She also added, "This hearing cannot be postponed nor have last-minute changes because I set it for today, and the lawyers accepted it".

All she knew to answer was NO, NO, NO. It is the job of any prosecutor in any country in the world.

Then I approached the judges' secretary, who treated me in a better way. She listened and said: "Perfect, lawyer!" She wrote my name and took it into account. At least, she was more polite.

The incredible thing about all this is that I had never seen this lawyer before, I didn't know where he came from. Many criminal lawyers appear on TV, in court or visiting their clients in prisons, but I had never seen him anywhere. It seemed strange to see that man sitting there. However, I did not see it wrong, on the contrary.

The funny thing is that after this case, I saw him many times in prisons and in courts. It was special to see him and every time I saw him, he smiled at me, and we greeted each other effusively.

The downside of being young is that people relate lack of experience to lack of competence. I had already had frictions with the criminal branch when I received my suitability as a lawyer. The day I got it, I received a call from an uncle who requested me to defend a cousin in prison. I accepted to help him, but I didn't do it for money. In fact, I decided not to charge him anything because it was my family, my blood and it hurt me a lot to see my uncle's suffering. I knew it was an opportunity to gain experience, which also tells a lot about my vocation as a lawyer. I took my cousin out of prison on a December 24th, which was one of the happiest day of my life. My greatest satisfaction was my uncle's happiness.

After a few weeks of receiving my suitability as a lawyer, I visited the prison and the court to present appeals in favor of my cousin. My first real criminal case was my cousin's one and getting him out of prison improved my self-esteem and gave me a lot of self-confidence in these cases.

Older people, regardless of their profession, have the tendency to neglect younger people. They feel that they have more experience and knowledge, which may be right, and they let you know it. The positive thing is that these people give you advice and sometimes their recommendations are precious. As a young person facing these circumstances, my job was to listen and to learn from the teachers.

Going back to the hearing, the recess was not yet over. I was one of all those who stayed in that room. When I looked at Ritesh, I saw that he was alone. He did not talk to anyone. The two lawyers separated from him and did not even talk to him. I could see that he looked surprised, and I noticed that he wanted to say many things.

While I was listening to the audience, I realized that I felt identified with him. I had memorized the four medications that were spoken about in the audience. I knew them perfectly. However, no one else in the room knew about the subject. They only saw a detainee in handcuffs that would be taken to trial.

In my country, I believe that after a certain age, many people know tramadol, since it is a medicine used for severe pain that resists common analgesics. Carisoprodol is completely unknown, and it is not sold in Panama.

I sat next to Ritesh and cheered him up by telling him: "I used to sell Tramadol, Carisoprodol and the four medications that were mentioned in the hearing."

Ritesh stared at me as impressed: Not only did I speak to him in English in a country where Spanish is spoken, but also I had sold the drugs for which he was accused. A young but multifaceted lawyer.

He replied with a sparkle of hope in his eyes: "Come and visit me tomorrow morning. We need to talk."

I returned to my position near the veteran lawyer and he said, with a big smile:

"Good job, that's how it is done".

The two lawyers looked well-positioned and prepared enough because they had been called on time. I did not even know that I would have an audience. Unlike them, I was not even dressed in a jacket and tie, which had lowered my spirit. But that man had encouraged me by giving me the impulse to talk.

"Don't worry, son, this client is yours, not only because you had the courage to stand up, but because the lawyers who are defending him have done a terrible defense".

He also said: "It is possible that this case will break out and appear in both national and international media. There are two big countries involved in this: the United States and India.

I heard part of what you talked about. I mean your knowledge of the medicines involved in this case." "God bless you son!"

After a few minutes, the three judges entered to give their decision of the control hearing.

I had my opinion about the lawyers' actions. Even if it was only the control audience, I think that their performance was very poor. There was not much foundation, they mentioned that the case had been pre-sented a short time before and they had not had enough time to study it.

The three judges left the recess and entered the room. Then, the judge-rapporteur said that after analyzing the situation, both parties,

The Public Prosecutor's Office and the client's defense, ordered Mr. Ritesh's arrest and would continue the extradition process in Panama.

The hearing finished, so the judges declared it adjourned. Ritesh got up from his seat, the policemen placed him the handcuffs and the shackles to lead him and take him back to prison.

This concludes the first hearing of Ritesh in the Supreme Court of Justice of Panama, the hearing of control or presentation.

CHAPTER 5

Lawyers Rained From Heaven

THE NEXT DAY, I WENT to visit Ritesh in the Preventive Cell, before he was sent to one of the main prisons in the country's capital.

I passed the first control and when I got to the second one, where the guards were taking my personal data, one of them said: "Today, three lawyers visited him, you are the fourth and, right now there is one talking to him. As soon as he leaves, I will let you go in, lawyer"

I knew there were two, but I did not know there was a third. What ability to get there so fast!

Ritesh had a vast group of lawyers to choose from. I was not alone. When this lawyer came out, I could see him and he was different from the two that were in the audience. But Ritesh had asked me to see him, so it had to be for a good reason.

When I took the phone, the only thing that separated us was the glass, thus we could talk face to face. Something that caught my attention was the swelling of his eyes, a signal that he had not slept for several days. His eyes were very irritated.

Ritesh greeted me. "Hello, how are you?"

"Great, thank you," I replied, but I did not ask him the question back for obvious reasons.

And he said smiling: "Today, you come better dressed."

Then, he proceeded: "You speak English much better than the three lawyers who came before you today. Two of them did not speak English at all, so I could understand nothing. You met one, I imagine because he just left"

I answered: "Yes, the three of them are out there, waiting to see what the other is doing."

My English is accented and the reason the other lawyers do not speak this language is that, unfortunately, the subject is not taught properly at public schools in our country. Therefore, most of the population does not speak it.

I was fortunate to study in one of the best private schools in the country. My mother; who holds a chair in Spanish, but is at this time retired; was a Spanish teacher there, so she enjoyed certain considerations. I can proudly say today that I studied at the oldest school in Panama, considered one of the best. However, nowadays new private schools with a great education system have emerged and the competition is getting stronger.

Ritesh kept asking me: "How did you see the other lawyers' participation? Because I think they said nothing. "But I liked what you did yesterday! You stood up and talked to the prosecutor, the secretary of the judges, and to me. You did more than the other two lawyers"

I remembered the veteran lawyer who was watching the audience, the strange but very kind man that urged me to act but left without giving me the opportunity to say goodbye to him that day.

To which I replied: "I cannot speak harmfully of any colleague for ethical reasons, but I would die in court for defending a client". Why did I tell him this? First, because I tried to make him understand that his lawyers did nothing and that my attitude would be different. Second, I knew it was the biggest case I had seen in my life. I have seen many things, but nothing like this. It was not only international but it also represented a different category. I was sure that I mastered the subject and that not even the judges and the prosecution knew about it as I did. I knew that the case would involve both national and international media. This case was a beauty. Indeed, I had never felt so self-confident.

As I had said before, the other lawyers were much older than I. One was at least fifty and the other two were over their sixties. With my thirty-two years and staying slim, the difference between them and I was too obvious.

None of the two lawyers had caused him a good impression because they had not played a good role in the audience, so he had to choose between the other one that was missing and me.

I have learned something in life: From ten businesses at least one will be for you and with that one is enough. You cannot force things or fight against destiny. If he chose me, I would give the best of me. If he didn't choose me, I had to move forward trusting that better things would come.

Regarding the other lawyers, I did not mean to backbite them. It was unnecessary. The client was not stupid and he knew that they did it wrong. Although many professionals from different careers and business people do it and it has worked for them, I dislike it. It is not my style. My strategy is always to give a positive response, making the client see that there may be something better, but without criticizing my colleagues' inaccuracy. However, from an honest point of view, their representation was not good.

Ritesh listened carefully and answered: "Everything you did in court for me was incredible, that's what I need. Deeply in my heart, I feel that you are the person who God is putting on my way to get me out of here so that I can return to my country, India.

"Find the best lawyer for me. A famous and respected lawyer whose trajectory impacts the judges. I'm sure you two would make a good team. Together, you will be stronger. You are too young to achieve it."

"I trust you. Bring me the number one, who will go to the front, who will speak before the judges. You will be number two."

It was an honor that he had chosen me as part of the lawyers to defend him, but why number two? Why couldn't I be number one? Well, at least he had chosen me, instead of the other three. I confirmed that being young has its advantages and its disadvantages.

In this world, there are things that seem a contradiction. For instance, everyone wants to be young. Many people fight to look young.

Others refuse to grow old or just never accept that they are not so young anymore, but age gives you experience and experience gives you more credibility.

He wanted to get out of prison. He knew about my knowledge on the subject since I had been linked to the business the previous years and knowing the subject made things easier, but he also wanted to make sure that he was hiring the best lawyer in the country, someone whose work and age demand credibility for us to make a team and ensure his release from prison. He did not want the best lawyer in the country to be alone. He wanted me to be with him because my knowledge was crucial to his case.

Sometimes, foreign people's cleverness seemed outstanding to me. Ritesh's intelligence surpassed that of the average people.

I went back home happy that day and I shared my daily experiences with my wife.

"Regina, I need the best lawyer, a famous lawyer, someone who impacts the judges only with his presence; he wants me to work together with a prestigious lawyer.

At that moment, Regina answered: "A famous lawyer here in Panama is Diego Molina, Michael's friend."

Michael is a dark-skinned gentleman from Bocas Del Toro, a province far away from the capital of Panama and near Costa Rica. I think that the fact of not being from the capital made him a unique person, noble and kind among other fantastic qualities. But, being so kind sometimes turned against him. He was a 60-year-old lawyer who worked with us for many years doing almost fifteen percent of the writings of our criminal cases. We had full confidence in him and his knowledge.

Michael was also very famous among lawyers. He had so much experience because he worked for over twenty-five years in the Public Ministry and was so efficient and successful that other lawyers had consulted him in different cases. However, he wasn't known in the media because the Public Ministry consumed most of his life. Michael had a great knowledge in criminal law, but since he had no reputation in the media, he was not who Ritesh was looking for.

I already had two lawyers in mind for Ritesh: A female friend of mine and Diego. The next day, I went to the preventive cell where Ambani was detained to tell him about these two lawyers. I started with the female lawyer because I knew she was great. What I had in mind was to make the best team for Ritesh.

My female lawyer was not as famous in the media as Diego, but she had worked over fifteen years as a prosecutor. I had already seen her in action and I did not know any criminal lawyer better than her in the country.

We met in a case a few years ago. She was a tall brunette woman with a well-shaped body and a strong character. We had offices in the same building, so we always saw each other. With a fashionable and sexy style, she used to catch the eyes of everyone. Sometimes when we were in the elevator, I felt she was watching me. Once, she invited me to have a coffee, but I never accepted because I was already married.

I was ready to talk to Ritesh about her in front of the glass, the place of the visitors at the preventive cell. I took the telephone and greeted him:

"Hello, Ritesh! How are you?"

Ritesh smiled at me and said: "Great! How about you?" He smiled a lot trying to be nice.

"As I told you yesterday, I like you. I feel it in my heart", he said to me again. "Apart from the fact that you said you have a good command of the medication issue, and you are the only one here who speaks English, but as I told you, you are too young. The lawyer to speak before the judges must be older and famous to impact the judges"

I already had that clear and I said: "I have a female lawyer who is a superb criminal attorney."

He said nothing about her. He only told me: "and the lawyer?" I felt some "male chauvinism" from his side, but it must be because of his country's culture. In my country, women can perform any type of job as effectively as men do or even better. We have even had a woman as President of the Republic. It made me very sad because he was neglecting a woman without knowing her capacity and professionalism.

I told him, "The male lawyer is a pure criminal attorney, among the best in the country. In fact, a very famous one." He looked directly to my eyes and told me: "It's okay. I want both of you to defend me". In that place, the time to speak was a little limited, so I had to leave quickly.

I met Diego through my friend Michael but I already knew him from television. I had seen him many times in high profile cases in the country. Actually, I had known him from TV since I was a child. He was a great veteran lawyer with a lot of experience, a specialist in criminal cases.

The next day, I called Michael to tell Diego about the situation and that we had the interest to work with him. Later, I spoke with Diego and he gladly accepted.

I posted the situation and explained that the client wanted to work with both. With me for two specific reasons: my knowledge about medicines and my mastery of the English language and with him for being the famous and recognized lawyer that would instill respect in front of the judges.

Before working together, and for Diego to impose his conditions to represent him, Ritesh had asked Diego to visit him.

Mumbai, India.
July 22nd, 2015
5:15 a.m.

Vivaan had already been waiting for his brother's call

The telephone rings.

It was Ritesh's call from Panama: "Hi, Vivian...I already found two lawyers. One of them is a young man who has a good command of the English language. Before becoming a lawyer, he worked for an online pharmacy and sold the four medicines that have to do with my case.

He will be the number two lawyer; he will bring me a powerful lawyer respected by the judges."

"I will fight in Panama. It will be a great fight against the United States. If I lose and they extradite me, it will be with my head held high and with dignity because I am a warrior."

He continued saying: "It is possible that my lawyers take this to the media and make a lot of noise." I'm not going to the United States, I'm innocent."

Vivaan could hardly whisper with a broken voice: "Ok, Ritesh, I support you."

CHAPTER 6

Diego Molina (The Charismatic and Famous Veteran Lawyer)

Panama, Panama City

WE SET UP A DAY to visit Ritesh in jail so that he and Diego knew each other. It had been a week, and Ritesh had already been transferred to the main prison.

Ritesh was transferred to "La Joya", a jail located in Panama City, two and a half hours from the city center. When you go to these facilities you have to spend almost all day to go through all the security checks. Each control takes from thirty to forty-five minutes, as far as it concerns the review. Considering that getting in and out both require going through the same controls, the time becomes even longer.

While Diego and I were heading there, we talked about trivial issues such as the weather condition. I confess that it is very hot place, apart from the fact that we were both wearing our formal outfit, which made the day even hotter.

We went in Diego's car. Diego was recognized as one of the most famous and charismatic lawyers in the country, and that day I could see why Ambani wanted someone like him.

As soon as we got to the prison, we walked towards the first control. Everyone seemed to know him. People talked to him and he made jokes with them. They also felt free to speak to him about any current topic

30

even though none of them knew him personally. As they knew him from TV, they treated him with camaraderie. However, they did not speak to me, they just greeted me respectfully. As the day went by, we continued going through the next controls, which were three in total.

When we passed the last checkpoint, we were ready to enter the prison, where we could see not only a large number of prisoners in the courtyard but also the soccer field, the rooms for family gatherings and the different pavilions.

While we were entering, several detainees shouted out his name: "Diego, Diego!!!". Others called him by his surname: "Molina!"

I felt as if I were walking next to an artist. Everyone wanted to talk to him. Some asked for money, others greeted him enthusiastically. Unlike him, I was unknown; nobody told me anything. It was as if I did not exist. I was very well dressed, but I was an invisible man next to Diego.

The visiting room was a tower. On the second floor and from the top, I could see Ambani, who could also hear everyone cheering at Diego. Even though he was not from this country, he had verified that I told him the truth. Ambani already knew that we were coming, so he was waiting for us.

Eventually, Ritesh got a cell phone to communicate with us with no problem. In fact, he called me almost every day. However, this did not last long. His own cellmates stole his cell phone making him believe that it had been lost in a requisition. He told me that he suspected a Colombian. Even though he got along with all the Colombians, there was one that he did not like very much. Although being in a place like that, I would suspect everyone, regardless the nationality.

He was in the cell group of foreigners because, in my country, the judicial system does not mix Panamanians with foreigners. There are prisoners from different nationalities in the cell of foreigners, but most of them are Colombians.

When we got there, he hugged me and introduced himself to Diego. They greeted each other. He looked enthusiastic and motivated; I was the translator since Diego does not speak English. I noticed they looked into each other's eyes for several seconds straight and forward. By gazing at Diego's eyes, Ambani wanted to discover if Diego was the person he was looking for. In the gaze, you will find what you can never read in the mind. A look can reflect the evilness, suffering, sadness, and pain of a person among many other things.

Diego told him: "I am Diego Molina, attorney at law. It's a pleasure to meet you". Diego was holding the daily newspaper. He opened a page where he appeared in the news that same day. And Diego said: "I am currently defending several policemen. I defended the government in a famous case."

We talked for several minutes. Then, Ambani told him: "Look, Henry knows a lot about the medications and I also find in him the strength I need for this case. You will be the powerful lawyer that impacts the judges, but Henry's knowledge is necessary, too."

"Do what you have to do", He proceeded. "If you have to take this to the press and that the whole country finds out, do it. I agree with what he said. Noise sometimes is necessary to pressure the judges.

Let me tell you something else, he proceeded: "Plan your strategy and your fees to get me out, and send it to my brother in India. I want you both and it's my final decision."

Then, we all embraced and Diego told him: "I will fight for your victory in the name of God" while raising Ritesh's arms in a sign of victory.

Diego approached me and whispered a question: "Do you know why I chose you? When you told me you would die for my case in court, I felt that you were the person sent by God to get me out of here."

Then, I said: "From the very beginning, I felt identified with you because I sold the same medicines. Knowing something that others ignore gives you a lot of security and I'm sure that neither the prosecutor nor the judges know what I know."

Finally, I expressed my gratitude to him for trusting me and we said goodbye.

After this, we left and went through the courtyard where the detainees were, and again, many people shouted Diego's name: Diego, Diego,

Molina!!! At that moment, Diego told me: "Colleague, I always bring several dollars to distribute but today I didn't, I feel sorry." And we kept walking to the door.

That visit in prison was positive. Ritesh was happy to have us as his lawyers, so I think we did it well. I told Diego, whose first impression was wonderful, about my personal satisfaction.

Diego and I had made a deal regarding our attorney fees. We would go fifty and fifty. We would be together in this from the beginning to the end.

Diego told me: "We have to find the file in court, analyze it and then give him our price"

CHAPTER 7

Ritesh's File

I WENT TO COURT EARLY to look for the file so I could get copies, and I met Diego's assistant. She would get copies to take to Diego. When both of us finished taking the copies, I left the courtroom. I had agreed to meet Diego the next day, once we had both read the file.

Even though I had my office, because he was older and because of the respect I had for him, I went to his office. The receptionist welcomed me and invited me to get in.

When I entered his office, his look and mine were of concern. The reason was too obvious. Diego had already warned me about it.

Diego: "Colleague, the case is serious. If I compare it with an illness, the patient has a deadly disease."

To which I replied: "Yes, colleague, the problem is serious."

Basically what the file said was:

An investigation leads to multiple charges against a citizen of India supplying drugs through an Internet pharmacy. This is Ritesh Ambani, a citizen of Mumbai, India; accused by a US grand jury on charges of mail fraud, drug trafficking conspiracy, conspiracy to import controlled substances from list IV and money laundering.

There were several charges in which Ritesh Ambani appeared as the only defendant.

According to the indictment, Ambani was a provider from India accused of selling medicines without allowed recipes through the internet to American consumers. He was charged with 10 counts of mail fraud, conspiracy to smuggle drugs, conspiracy to import controlled substances from list IV and two counts of money laundering.

Except for conspiracy charges, each of which is punishable by five years in prison, all other charges would have a maximum penalty of 20 years. Each charge of money laundering carries a maximum fine of 500,000 USD, (five hundred thousand dollars) while 250,000 USD (two hundred and fifty thousand dollars) is the maximum fine for the remaining charges. Under the Federal Sentencing Guidelines, the sentence imposed would be based on the seriousness of the crimes and the prior criminal history.

An assistant prosecutor was processing this case on behalf of the United States government.

The Ministry of Foreign Affairs was the liaison in charge of deciding whether the extradition of our client to the United States was viable or not, along with the three magistrates of the Supreme Court of Justice of Panama.

The detective who was carrying the case that brought Ritesh to Panama had deceived him. When he arrived in Panama, he was detained; he maintained an extradition request to the United States.

Once Diego saw the file, he told me his legal fees, and said: "Henry, as I do not speak English and the client is yours, take care of the agreement with his brother."

The idea was to prepare a team of four people to defend the case. The specialist of extradition cases, Michael, by Diego's decision, who wanted him in the case, Diego and I.

It was a powerful team and Diego's fees were even higher than I thought.

CHAPTER 8

Ritesh believed in his lawyers

A VETERAN HAS A LOT of experience, he uses wise strategies that he has develoved through the years; cases in which he had to intervene. Likewise a Young man shows his talents, his aspirations, his strenghts, his desirees to put in practice his knowledge in cases like this. Like all young people with aspirations, I had a lot of desires and many dreams. I already had a family, a one-year-old baby, and I made my promise to Ritesh one day, by looking him in the eyes, that I would die for him in court. This was the most serious case I had had so far. He had already decided he wanted us and nobody else.

A lawyer must keep professional secrecy. In all my other cases I kept it, this case was not the exception. I always remained loyal to the trust and confidentiality of my clients, not only for respect to my profession, but also for respect to my human essence and values.

This case was not only special but fascinating. From its inception, I perceived what I had never felt the same emotion in any other case. It was also historic, impressive. So many elements together that make it remain in history and, the most important thing was that it was against one of the greatest potentials all over the world: the United States.

I only expected the call from Ritesh's brother, a young man I did not know and had never seen, only talked with him by phone. For a moment, I thought that the amount Diego asked for was too high, but I remembered when Ambani told me that one of the four lawyers was charging him twenty thousand USD and that he laughed because he had considered it too cheap. He told me: "Henry, how is he going to charge me only twenty thousand USD for this case, a case so serious and big?"

Then, I realized that the amount suggested by Diego was much more adjusted to reality since it was necessary to cover the extradition specialist's fees, those of Michael, and what the extradition process entailed, which could be extended to over one year.

CHAPTER 9

The Negotiation

THE NEXT DAY, I RECEIVED the call from Ritesh's brother. I was ready to give him the amount suggested by Diego.

The telephone rings:

"Hi, I'm Vivaan, Ritesh's brother"

"Hi, Vivaan, how are you?"

Fine, thank you. He replied.

Vivaan's voice sounded like that of a very affected man, the voice of a beaten person who was suffering a lot. "Look, Henry, I have spoken with my brother. I am in charge of coming into an agreement with you, and I will support him in everything. Since he is detained, everything is difficult for him."

I said-- It's fine.

"Well, now I would like you to tell me about your fees and whom we would sign the contract with."

Diego had given only his fees and had left me in charge of communicating with them because of my mastery of the language.

There is a pause...Then, Vivaan tells me: "Well, Henry, my brother wants both of you. What are we talking about? Tell me your fees to talk to my brother and my family."

After I gave him the number, I noticed a sudden silence. Then, he said: "I will talk to my brother and my family. I'll call you tomorrow"

The next day, Vivaan called me again very early. Even though He was in India, He went into Google to see Panama's time zone and was already managing it well. And he told me:

"Henry, I talked to my family and my brother and we agree on it, but we need a discount of thirty-three percent."

I said: "Let me talk with Diego to take a decision."

I spoke with Diego and he agreed on the discount, so he urged me to proceed.

It was so unexpected that I did not believe it. I knew it was a high amount. I was willing to give my best to avoid this man's extradition. He had believed in me and I would not disappoint him. I also promised to be vigilant that Diego did his job as expected.

The next day, when I was about to start the contract, I received another call from Vivaan. He told me: "Hello, Henry, how are you?"

"Fine, Vivaan, how about you?" I answered

"I feel well, thanks", he replied in a very low voice.

"Look, Henry: We will ask you one last favor in this negotiation. We want you to give us a fifty percent discount. Look, it's a lot of money. If it's done, we'll sign the contract tomorrow."

They were asking for a lower price again. I answered: "Well, Vivaan let me talk to Diego, to see what he says about this. I'll inform you."

I called Diego again:

"Good evening, colleague! Ritesh's brother is asking us for an additional 50-percent discount on our fees."

The only thing that Diego told me was: "They are merchants, they never lose."

When I asked him what to do, he answered without hesitating: "We will accept. No problem"

I called Vivaan and told him we had accepted upon the condition that there would not be any other discount.

I knew it was a good deal anyway because even with the fifty percent discount it still represented good business. Although if he asked for a seventy-five percent discount, I do not know Diego, but I would have accepted because I knew that the case had many inconsistencies and that we could do great things. Besides, winning it would be the best basis for any other extradition case, which was my vision.

The contract was ready, I only had to change the percentages, and I would do it on behalf of my law firm, not on behalf of Diego's. The reason? The client was mine, not Diego's.

I sent the contract to Vivaan, and that was exactly the observation he made.

I noticed seriousness in his voice when he said: "I did not know that I had to send the money to you, or to your company, I thought we would send it to Diego because he is the main lawyer. I will talk to my brother and then I'll call you."

My answer showed him that I didn't have any objection at all: "Good, ask your brother".

He spoke with his brother, who told him that everything was fine, that he could send it and that there was no problem. He saw nothing else in the contract. Since he agreed on everything, I sent it to him; he signed it, authenticated it and returned it signed by DHL.

He told me: "In a few days, I will send fifty percent to start."

Ritesh was happy. I felt calm, and I was clear of the great responsibility I had.

In countries like Panama, defending a detainee is a sensitive issue. You have to act honestly and not cheat the client. Never tell him that you will take him out, or make promises that you won't be able to fulfill. Tell him that you will fight, that the case is tough, and that he will have the best defense. When you promise that you will release the client and do not do it, you are in serious troubles. Many lawyers have even died because of this.

A contract does not guarantee freedom, but a good defense based on a legal basis, and with all the willingness to do the best job is a good guarantee for any customer. The lawyer who guarantees freedom takes a risk unless he knows the judge because this is a delicate matter. In addition, extradition cases are the most difficult according to statistics.

Sometimes people criticize and judge lawyers, but those who are honest professionals and do a good job sometimes do not have the luck to be valued.

If there is something that I have learned in the criminal area of this career is that the client of criminal cases is the most ungrateful one. You take him out of prison, but sometimes he neither thank you nor pay you. I say this because, before this case, I had several such incidents.

Despite being young as Ritesh said, I had already attended several criminal cases and, because of bad experiences with customers who did not pay, I prefer not to see so many of these cases now because I distrust them.

I remember once I came to defend a client that had been apprehended at the airport with two hundred thousand dollars hidden in a suitcase. All the people in customs at the airport told me that this was for drugs and that he would be prosecuted for money laundering. The man that I defended used to tell me: "I have done this many times, my group has a lot of money, and we will pay you whatever you want." I put a price to start and his answer was always the same: "Do not worry, we have money." I was a recent graduate of the university. Even though I put a price to start, whenever I asked him, he gave the same answer. He lied all the way, but I accepted the deal, prepared his defense and defended him in the investigation, and that man had the best defense. Unfortunately, he paid nothing. I felt used and I learned to distrust criminal cases.

But Ritesh Ambani's was a different case. He wanted to avoid being extradited and he trusted my capacity to achieve it. We already had his file, a copy for each lawyer, Diego and I. I was already studying it to see what I could find.

CHAPTER 10

Something Unexpected

THE FIRST CALL I RECEIVED that day was from Vivaan:

"Henry, Good Morning! As it is so much money, can we do it in two money transfers with a week difference between both?

To which I responded: "No problem, for me it's fine, go ahead."

Vivaan sent the money, which came from an account under Ritesh Ambani's name. It surprised me how much money these people handled.

I got involved in that case as nobody else; I read many extradition cases that I got in court.

Suddenly, and after some advance, something unexpected happened. Diego did not answer the phone. He disappeared. We kept the money in our corporate account, but Diego had not received his part. Desperate, I called my friend Michael to see if he had news of him, but he told me that he had not heard from him either.

I did not know how to tell Ambani's brothers that I did not know where Diego was. It had been three days and nothing was known about him. Until the moment that Ambani suspected and Vivaan, who was in India told me: "Henry, how about Diego? I have not heard from him."

I said:" Look, he's seeing a famous court case, so he will be absent for a few days. But then, he will be back with us."

Two more days passed and we knew nothing about him. I wondered where Diego was. My concern was not so much about the money or our business, now it was about his life. I wondered if he was alive or dead.

We had no news of Diego, I went to his own office to talk to his secretary and she told me that she knew nothing about him, except that he had gone to the countryside, to another province. She also told me that Diego's wife would come in the afternoon and that she would ask her.

It worried me, if not even his secretary knew where he was, it was a serious matter.

Vivaan called again and said: "Henry, the second payment is ready, but... what do you know about Diego?"

I said: "Look, I already talked to the secretary and he will be with us soon, but right now he is attending another big case."

He almost did not let me finish saying the last words when he interrupted in an energetic tone: "Henry, understand, we also have a serious problem. I won't make the second transfer until I talk to Diego. I have to know he's alive and that he will continue with my brother's case."

I told him. "OK, no problem."

The next day in the morning, Diego called me:

"Hello, Henry, how are you?" Listening to him was incredible happiness for me.

I said: "Diego, where are you?"

"I'm here in my office." He answered.

And I explained the situation: "Ambani's brother sent me part of the money, but he won't send the second part until he hears your voice over the phone as evidence that you are alive."

To which Diego responded: "Come to my office, where we will talk to him so he can see that I am alive, and we are ready to start"

Diego confessed that he had to solve family problems, his father-in-law tried to commit suicide and he had been desperate about that situation.

From his office, we could talk to Vivaan. He felt thrilled, and said: "I will make the second transfer right away." They had already transferred two-thirds of the total amount; the remaining third would be sent after Ambani's freedom.

That same day, I sent his fifty percent to Diego. He received it and told me: "These people fulfilled their promise, now it is our turn. Let's get to work!"

Ritesh Signs us the Power of Attorney to Represent Him

FRIDAY, August 14ᵗʰ, 2015. PANAMA, PANAMA CITY.

THE FIRST STEP TO DEFEND a detainee is to draft the power of attorney or authorization to defend him in court.

I made the power of attorney and sent it to Diego's mail so he could check it, see if it satisfied him, and make any arrangements if it was necessary. He considered everything was ok, so with his secretary's help, he entered his logo and made the modifications according to his style, printed and signed it. Then, he asked me to stop by the office whenever I wanted because he had given the secretary instructions to give it to me. And so I did, I picked it up and signed it.

Basically, what the power of attorney said was that Diego Molina was the main lawyer, and I was the secondary lawyer representing the client at the Supreme Court of Justice in Panama. As soon as we entered it in the Court, this new power of attorney would revoke or eliminate the previous one that the first lawyers had entered. We were inside the case. The next day, I went to jail by myself, this time without Diego, to get Ritesh's signature.

Ritesh used to call me almost every day. He did not have much time to talk, only a few minutes, but he took advantage to say everything he could.

When I got to jail, he was waiting for me. He was eager to see me. This time, we were in the same room, sitting face to face.

"Thanks for coming"

He made a pause and said: "I would like to make a suggestion. The first day you went to see me, you were not wearing a suit. When you go to see a detainee the first time, you must make a good impression; you should have worn a suit that day.

When I answered, I noticed Ritesh made some strange head movements while listening to me. It was sometimes a swing from one side to another, like a headshake (wobble) and at other times he nodded his head. After investigating about it on the internet, I discovered that some people from India do these movements imitating a cobra, as a kind of flattery, respect, and approval showing agreement and interest towards what you are saying. It was something new for me, something completely different from our Latin culture.

Being so young and not wearing a suit made him feel insecure about my professionalism and that's why he asked me to look for the best lawyer in the country. Or maybe he wanted the best lawyer from the beginning. That is something only he knows.

I explained to him that when Amil called me, I did not have to attend any client at the office. When he called, I was not dressed to visit any person, but my experience tells me that when a lawyer doesn't attend an unexpected case at the moment he is being called, the client soon looks for another lawyer. If I had gone back to my house to change clothes, another lawyer would have come in.

"How do I look, now?" I asked him ironically.

"You look very elegant today, Henry," he said laughing.

Ritesh was a very attentive and pleasant person. His eyes only reflected the sadness he was going through, but I understood his situation and I was there to support him.

It was something he understood. I was acting not only for business but for loyalty. If I wanted to help him, I had to get him out of prison and avoid that extradition at all costs. He had believed in me above three other lawyers and this was enough to struggle for him in court. As I mentioned earlier, I had already had family members detained, so I knew about this feeling and how much a family suffers. Having this experience, one understands that it is something serious. Maybe that is why I do not take every criminal case. Freedom is the most precious thing a person has. It is a serious commitment. If I did not consider it seriously, I wouldn't have accepted the case.

In the middle of the conversation, Ritesh offered me water or soda, which they have for sale in prisons and I accepted a bottle of water. While drinking the water and talking, he asked for the same bottle and from there he drank, too. This is not common in our Latin-American culture, at least not in my country, Panama. People here drink from their own glasses and bottles. We do not share these things with anybody except close family members such as parents, siblings, and couples.

Once with the power of attorney signed, I asked him some questions that came from both Diego and I. They were all answered and I took notes of everything he said. After that, we both looked at each other. I knew it was time for me to listen to him. His eyes got wet as he told me the story. I think Diego should have also been there to hear it by himself and not that I passed it on, but for him, it was sometimes complicated, because of the other big cases he had.

Ritesh looked at the sky as if asking why. Then he lowered his head and looked to one side as if finding the words and said:

"The judges at the Court have to know how an Interpol officer acting as a businessman contacted me, establishing messages and making promises to do great business. So, to gain my trust, he gave me an order of seven hundred and eight ($708) USD, and then he tricked me into coming to Panama because it is a good country for tourism and for good business opportunities."

"We have exported these drugs legally after they were approved by the India FDA. (Ministry of Health of India)If I had committed any fault or crime, I should have been arrested in India, since the USA has an extradition treaty with India."

"Why did he seduce me, inviting me to Panama, trapping me in a hotel and arresting me?What a fool I was!—He started crying— "that agent from the United States deceived me. He is smarter than I, he cheated me, how could I be so foolish to believe him and come to Panama! I fell into his trap and now I'm in jail."

"Henry, in my family something like this had never happened. If my mother finds out, she will have a heart attack. What has happened is a disgrace to my family."

And he told me the details of his business. I shared with Ritesh for a period of over two hours. That day, I realized who Ritesh Ambani was. He was a great person, contrary to what the charges against him suggested, who was going to be judged unfairly. I was convinced that he was innocent.

The last thing he said was: "Henry, because of all I'm going through, the ones that worry me the most are my mother and my ten-year-old son because he's growing up, and he understands everything. I've disappointed him and I feel sad about that; my family is alone, without me.,"

To which I replied: "Have faith, let's fight together. Do not martyr yourself thinking about that, be positive Ritesh. You have a process coming soon and we will defend you. I am with you, you are not alone, and remember that you also have Diego, one of the best lawyers,"

I was astonished at his answer: "Henry, you are greater than Diego,"

CHAPTER 12

The Details of Ritesh's Business

A LITTLE CALMER, RITESH CONTINUED venting, being honest, and telling me things as they happened: "Henry, one of my businesses is an online pharmacy. I sell drugs to several countries, not only to the United States. But if this is a bad thing, I do not want to do it any longer. I can devote myself to my other businesses, which have nothing to do with this. I can do business in other countries; it does not have to be only with the United States."

"I'll explain to you, Henry: I sold medicines to an American who had his pharmacy in Costa Rica, outside the United States. I was the exporter, he was the importer. He was arrested and forced to say my name. In addition, he bought from many other vendors in India. I have committed no crime. The drugs are not fake. They are generic drugs. In India, recognized brand laboratories manufactured them. The only error is that the medicines did not have the prescription, but this is not my job. It's not the exporter's, but the importer's job; therefore, the exporter does not have to be detained,"

After a long, deep breath, he continued. "A bad person deceived me. When I met with this agent in Panama, he was accompanied by another person, who didn't mistreat me the way he did. When I introduced myself, I told them that I had brought a present from India, and I gave it to them. While he refused it by saying he wasn't interested in any gifts, the other one kindly accepted it.

About to burst into tears, Ritesh recalled the ominous moment when the agent said: "I'm from the government of the United States. This is a covert operation." Then, with a lump in his throat, he said almost sobbing: "I was shocked. The world came over me. It is the worst experience I've ever had in my life. Later, I was out in the police car and I was arrested. I think I will hardly trust people again after this. This man posed as a client, and he persistently asked me to sell him regulated medicines. I told him I could not sell him that kind of medication. In fact, I never sold him what he asked for. I sold him the softest because I could not commit that crime."

That afternoon, I felt eager to go back home, to hug my son and my wife. I have always valued what a family represents, but Ritesh's experience had made me even more aware of it. I thought about my wife and how she has supported me in everything by giving me her advice and recommendations especially in Ritesh's case.

The next day, when the power had all the signatures requested (Diego's, Ritesh's and mine), I went to the second room of the Court accompanied by Diego to present this power of attorney. Immediately, the previous power of attorney was revoked. From that moment on, we were Ritesh's new lawyers. We had a great responsibility. That afternoon, I thanked God for the opportunity he had given me.

Something that I have to recognize of Indian clients is that they are very serious in their commitments; I have had several in different cases. When they tell you the business is going on, it's one hundred percent sure.

Entering the power of attorney to defend Ritesh in court until that moment was the greatest thing, just by remembering it, beautiful memories come to mind.

Before sleeping that night, I was talking with my wife about it, who, after listening to the whole story, couldn't help showing her compassion for Ritesh.

"Poor Ritesh!" I feel sorry about him. His story is very touching."

To which I replied: "He is tormented with everything: the food, the language."

"Henry, if he has done something wrong, he is already paying."

To which I responded: "I think he already paid for it, he told me he is in hell. And he does not understand why God has allowed him to be there. But you know something, Regina? The guy is a good man"

And she asked me: "Do you think so?

"Yes, Regina, I talked to him. Now, he is suffering, I can see it in his eyes". That night, I could hardly sleep thinking about the case.

CHAPTER 13

A Covert Operation

MANY PEOPLE IN THE UNITED States were buying different drugs online without knowing their source. For example, Viagra. For many men, it was less embarrassing to buy it online since they did not need a prescription. Likewise, people could buy all kinds of medicines without a prescription, such as pain medication.

These non-prescription drugs regularly came from other countries, but these websites mostly came from Asian countries such as India. They were sent from India not only to the United States but to the United Kingdom, Australia, and Africa.

The United States government was pressuring several countries for this problem.

9 MONTHS BEFORE

The government of the United States was facing a war difficult to fight. It had closed hundreds of online pharmacies, but new ones were open every day. It was an epidemic on the internet and it had become a big health problem even outside the internet in several countries.

But the worst for online pharmacies is that, due to lack of knowledge about opioids, they had been classified as an epidemic called opioids epidemic.

Opioids are a different class of strong pain drugs that include Oxycodone, Oxycontin, Percocet, Hydrocodone (Vicodin), and

Fentanyl. But one of these, fentanyl, was causing many deaths per year, almost 55,000 in 2015 and 64,000 in 2016. It was produced in China and trafficked on the streets. This ignited the alarm of the government which was determined to stop it. Those who came from India had nothing to do with these from China, but they were not well seen.

Once I had the file, I started investigating who was the covert agent who arrested Ritesh. I put his name on Google and I found the following information:

John Palmieri was a retired police officer and currently a covert agent of a major United States institution. He was following up on Ritesh and communicating with him by email. Not only did he carry the case of Ritesh, but he carried the case of other Indians who were engaged in the same activity.

At that moment, I remembered one of Amil's phone call, when he told me:

"Give me your email. I want to send you the email exchanges between Ritesh and the covert agent. What is happening is unfair."

I had received the mail but had not downloaded the attachment yet. However, when I arrived at the office, I sat down at my computer table, opened the mail and the attached file and read it. There were 57 pages, a complete exchange of e-mails that lasted four months and started this way:

Wednesday
[06:16 AM] Ambani International has shared the contact details with Roger Donovan. ***
[5:06:35 AM] Ambani International: Yes, Roger
[5:06:38 AM] Ambani International: It's Ritesh
[3:36:18 PM] Ambani International: Hello
[5:07:15 PM] Roger Donovan: Hi, Ritesh, how are you?

[5:07:48 PM] Ambani International: Good!

[5:07:58 PM] Ambani International: Have you seen my answer?

[5:08:04 PM] Roger Donovan: I just read your email. I have to leave for a few hours and when I return I will send you an answer. I am pleased that you have seen my application.

[5:09:09 PM] Ambani International: I'm so impressed your e-mail is detailed

[5:09:15 PM] Ambani International: so clear

[5:09:20 PM] Ambani international: focused

[5:10:48 PM] Roger Donovan: Only standard in the USA. If you want to manage a successful business, it is easy to distinguish people who can do things from those who cannot do it.

[5:11:29 PM] Ambani International: 0k

[5:11:34 PM] Roger Donovan: I will leave. I'll send you an e-mail when I return.

[5:11:40 PM] Ambani International: Ok

[5:11:45 PM] Ambani International: Bye for now

[5:11:46 PM] Ambani International: Thanks

[11:53:56 PM] Roger Donovan: I just sent you an e-mail

Thursday

[7:24:18 AM] Ambani International: OK, I'll see it

[5:32:09 PM] Roger Donovan: Good morning. Did you read my last e-mail?

[5:32:39 PM] Ambani International: You will receive an e-mail in five minutes

[5:36:20 PM] Roger Donovan: 0k

[5:37:55 PM] Ambani International: I just sent it

[5:38:01 PM] Ambani international: Please, update your mail

[5:42:55 PM] Roger Donovan: I could only read your e-mail. I have to take the children to school, and then I'll get in touch with you, thanks.

Friday

Roger Donovan: Was there anything else we could mention about the brands you're offering?

[5:06:14 PM] Ambani International: I'm thinking of sending you some pills from bigger brands from manufacturers like SUNPHARMA, GLENMARK, AND INTAS

He was offering SUNPHARMA, which is one of the five largest brands of generic drugs in the world, approved by the FDA in fifteen countries in Europe (including Germany, France, and England), the United States, Canada, Brazil, Asia, and Africa.

The second brand that was offered was also generic, approved by the FDA and with a presence in India, the United States, Europe, and Latin America.

The third brand was also global and generic, approved by the FDA and with a global presence.

[5:06:50 PM] Ambani International: The prices would be much more than the brands I offered you

[5:07:24 PM] Ambani International: But if any medication of the brand I offer you is not good enough, we can opt for the big brands

[5:07:57 PM] Ambani International: I will receive samples along with the order of the big brands and I will send them to you FREE with the shipment.

[5:08:15 PM] Ambani International: How many pills are good enough to analyze? ... about a hundred pills?

[5:09:12 PM] Roger Donovan: Two things. One, how much more? The most important thing for me is the quality. I cannot have medicines that are fragile, poorly stamped, etc. Sending some of the best things is a great idea. I need a few to try.

[5:09:19 PM] Ambani International: Although I am sure of the quality of the products I have offered you, I want to be more secure.

[5:09:56 PM] Roger Donovan: I agree. It's safer to send everything and let me review it. Please let me know the price difference for the other medications.

I will email you the price list with these big brands in a few minutes.
[5:12:00 PM] Roger Donovan: OK, thanks.
[5:54:26 PM] Ambani International: It will take me one day while I wait for the prices of the big brands, I will respond soon.

Saturday
[4:33:20 PM] Roger Donovan: "Any luck finding the other Celebrex?"
[4:34:43 PM] Ambani International: "Yes, I tried it everywhere"
[4:35:04 PM] Ambani International: "It is not possible to have blue/white similar to COBIX-200mg,"
This conversation coincided with what Ritesh had told me, that the undercover agent was asking for stronger and more risky controlled medications and that he would not send them.
Celebrex is a medication regulated by the federal government. It has complications and risks for the consumer and must have a medical prescription.
[4:35:39 PM] Roger Donovan: OK. Cobix will not manufacture without your name in the capsule?
[4:36:13 PM] Ambani International: They will not
[4:36:16 PM] Ambani International: off course not
Putting Cobix's name on the mark would go from generic to fake medicine, and the undercover agent was asking him to put the name on the capsule.
Ritesh replies: "The laboratory will not do that."
From the first sentence that I read about this undercover agent, it brought back many memories: "John Palmieri was a retired police officer and an undercover agent of an important institution in the United States."
I think people who are already retired and continue working should be evaluated for the work they do or should be removed from the system because, in my country, I have connected with accountants and retired financiers who continue working, but do not follow the rules, and do what they think is right.

I have always thought young people should be given an opportunity. A retired person who insists on working but is doing a bad job not only harms the country but also takes away the opportunity for a young person to develop.

This was a retired police officer, although it is true he should have more judicial knowledge than an accountant, for example, he is not a lawyer and does not know the laws.

There was a name in the conversation that caught my attention. Ritesh had told me about this person, who was the American who operated from Costa Rica, but who was the importer in the United States of the goods that he sent him. The name of this person was Thomas and I could confirm it through the following conversation.

Roger Donovan:	Why do you think Thomas got in trouble?
Ritesh:	Thomas did not have a license to import, and he did not pay the huge tariffs on the product before he put them into his warehouse.
	Sure enough, there was a Thomas, and it came up in the conversation and this agreed with what Ritesh had told me. The conversation continued:
Roger Donovan:	Even with my license, these are kind of things you are sending to the United States, a country that does not currently allow the entry of these drugs. Why do you think customs was intercepting the packages you sent Thomas?
	This confirms that Ritesh was not an importer. He was an exporter.
	The undercover agent claimed that Ritesh was shipping from India to the United States. This makes Ritesh an exporter and makes Thomas the importer.
	I think since the undercover agent mentioned Thomas' name, Ritesh was cautious and did not want to enter the United States.

The agent had confirmed two things:

1. Thomas had gotten into trouble
2. The packages he was sending to Thomas had been intercepted by customs.

For being cautious and not wanting to enter the United States, his capture had to be prepared in Panama. According to the undercover agent, the business had to be closed in a personal meeting, and since Ritesh did not want to enter the United States, it had to be in another country.

Roger Donovan:	My runner finally answered to me about his trip. He said he had a meeting scheduled in Panama in July. You would like to end our meeting at the same time. Do you see any problem with the meeting in Panama? We can hold a Saturday / Sunday meeting as requested. Probably, July 11th and 12th
Ambani International:	Panama would be fine.
Ambani International:	Time also seems good to me.
Roger Donovan:	Perfect, do you need some kind of visa to travel there? Is there enough time for you?
Ambani International:	I have to apply for a visa, which I think should be no problem; I will check this on Monday with travel agents.
Roger Donovan:	Re-contact me next week, once you have contacted a travel agent to see if we advance from there.
Ritesh Ambani:	Hello, a travel agent answered and sent me the requirements to apply for a tourist visa to enter Panama.
Roger Donovan:	Okay, Didn't they ask for a blood test? Hahaha! Just kidding.

Ritesh Ambani:	No, no. They asked for the normal things for this type of visa. We Indians are accustomed to getting this type of requirements for tourist visas.
Roger Donovan:	Ok, I will talk to the broker and I'll send you the exact date. I'm sure it will be around July 11.
Roger Donovan:	I have to take the children to school. We'll check it later; let me know if you need anything else.

Ritesh's visa was approved to enter Panama, and both continued communicating about what would be the meeting in Panama.

Ritesh Ambani:	The problem with going to Panama is that I have to stop in the USA, Europe, Canada or Australia at least one day and then go to Panama.
Roger Donovan:	The meeting is critical, especially for the sending and processing. I dislike picking up packages through the post office.
Ritesh Ambani:	Hello, the visa from Panama will take me a long time, which is why I have applied for a visa in France. France's is ready in three days. Nationals of India can travel to Panama with a visa from the United States or Europe, and that of France takes less time. So I'll be in Paris for a day or two and then I'll travel to Panama.
Roger Donovan:	I thought you had a European visa.
RiteshAmbani:	It's expired; I've traveled to Europe many times.

Ritesh, as he mentioned, was a small salesman. There were many people more important than he, and because he wanted to impress he said he had traveled to Europe. Indeed, he had never been to Europe, but he wanted to look like a great businessman.

The day was approaching.

Roger Donovan:	When do you leave India? I leave on Tuesday.

Ritesh Ambani: No, I'm going out today. Because I have to stay in Paris for two days, I leave Paris in the morning and arrive in Panama on the evening of the fourteenth.

Roger Donovan: Do you have any plans in Paris? I've never been there, but I've heard that it's very nice.

Ritesh Ambani: Yes, I will stay near the Eiffel Tower, and then I will go on a city tour.

Two Days Later
July 14th, 2015

Ritesh Ambani: I'm at Paris airport and I'm going to Panama in one hour.
I will arrive at 6 p.m. and I will be at the hotel where we will meet around 7 p.m.

The Directors of Pharmacies and Drugs of the Ministry of Health of Panama have announced over the past two years that generic medicines are as effective as the original ones and that it is a fallacy to say that generic products are not reliable. They show that these drugs before going to the market or to the pharmacies of the public health entities have been evaluated by the National Directorate of Pharmacies and Drugs, who granted a sanitary registry because they showed safety and efficacy. Besides, their quality has been proved through the studies carried out by the Analysis Institute of the University of Panama.

In the United States in 2017, more generic drugs were approved than ever before.

By the end of 2017, The United States FDA (Food and Drug Administration) had given its approval for seven hundred and sixty-three new versions of generic drugs, more than in 2016.

But there was another problem for Ritesh. In recent months, there was a drug that was not coming from India, but it was ending many lives in China. The drug that was in the storm's eye is called Fentanyl. Although it was sold mainly in the streets and not in online pharmacies, it was being classified within the opioid group.

It was called Epidemic Opioid, and it has claimed the lives of thousands of people in the United States.

CHAPTER 14

Preparing for the First Court Hearing

Friday, September 4, 2015

I WAS IN MY OFFICE when received a call from Diego: "Colleague, the prosecutor called me. She has Ritesh's suitcase and wants to give it to us. Can we meet tomorrow?"

"Ok, buddy, we're going in my car. Is 9:00 a.m ok for you?

"It seems good," he told me and we set our mind to it.

We entered the prosecutor's office related to International affairs. The receptionist welcomed us and asked us to move forward where the assistant attorney of the prosecutor attended us.

When Diego speaks his charisma is noted by everyone. That day, I was impressed. I could see the respect and the admiration in the receptionist's eyes for dealing with someone so well-known. She kept silent just listening to him. I still remember that look.

Once more, I confirmed what Ritesh was looking for. A few minutes later, the prosecutor entered, greeted us with a smile and handed us the suitcase, and a document that we signed as proof of delivery.

We said goodbye, and that's how we got out of the prosecution.

Back in my car, Diego asked me:

"Colleague, have you read the file?"

"About three times," I replied.

"Have you found anything?

"Several things", was my response.

"Well, you will keep finding more and more new things as the days go by. I have also found several of them."

For me, there was no other more important case at the moment and I said: "Dude, I have left all my other works with my assistant. At this moment, I am focused on Ritesh. He is my priority now, and I will treat him as if he were a family member."

And Diego responded with a lot of motivation: "Yes, they trust us. We have to comply, too. We will request the precautionary measure."

"I think it's a good idea, lawyer, I answered.

And so, we said goodbye to each other.

That same day in the afternoon, I received a call from Ritesh. He and his brother communicated with me and not with Diego. It was difficult for them because sometimes they wanted to talk to Diego. T I had to transmit everything to both. Ritesh's calls were always at almost the same time. He could use the phone, at 6:30 p.m.

An incoming call from Ritesh; 6:30 pm

"Hi Henry, did you receive the payment my brother made?"

"Yes Ritesh, thank you, we are already working on your case."

"Henry, please, get me out of this hell."

"I'm fighting for that. I have left everything else to focus on your case along with Diego"

I continued listening to him: "My brother who is in India is arranging his visa to travel to Panama, but the first one who will arrive in Panama on my behalf is a trusted friend of mine, named Amil,"

The only one Diego and I knew was Ritesh, we did not know anyone else since they were all in India.

It's okay I said, "We're waiting for them here."

Two days passed, which I took to study the file completely. Each time I found more and more information in our favor. I was determined not to let this man's extradition. I already had my writing with all the violations, inconsistencies, and points from the file in our favor.

On Thursday, I met with Diego. He had invited Michael. Among the three, Diego was the captain of the ship, the one in front by Ritesh's decision. I contributed with my ideas and so did Michael.

We were all three talking about the case. I had a point so strong that I told them at once:

"The four drugs that appear in the file as those that were admitted to the United States by Ritesh are Tramadol, Carisoprodol, Sildenafil, and Tadalafil. In the file, The USA government labeled them as narcotics and as a crime under the category of narcotics trafficking conspiracy. Why? Because this is how you can get extradition since the new treaties were created to combat narcotics. But guess what? None of the four medications turn out to be narcotics, I tell you, I sold the four medications when I worked in the call center, and they are making them look like narcotics only to get the extradition."

At that moment, Diego answered:

"The solution to this is very simple, lawyer: The Ministry of Health in Panama and the Department of Pharmacies and Drugs. They are the ones who can tell if these are narcotics or not."

Diego suggested me going to The Pharmacies and Drugs Department to get four certifications that proved that none of these drugs are narcotics. Excellent idea!

Diego looked at me and said, "We will beat them out with what you have, the first thing we're going to do is request the precautionary measure."

Diego had given me a tremendous idea. The next day, at 8:00 am, I went to the Department of Pharmacies and Drugs of the Ministry of Health. I spoke with the Director of regulated medicines of the Republic of Panama. I told her about these four medications, and I asked her if they were narcotics.

She answered: "Lawyer, none of these medications are considered narcotics."

Then, I requested her signed certification as a piece of evidence for our case.

When I left this office, I felt excited. I called Diego at once to tell him the good news and he said: "Come to my office, tell me all the details. Do you have something to do now? Can you come to my office now?"

Upon arriving at the office, Diego and Michael were waiting for me.

Diego welcomed me with an explosion of joy: "What you got today is very useful, lawyer- Let's use it as proof. We will request the hearing so that they grant us the precautionary measure in favor of Ritesh. I'm going to prepare the document, and I'll send it to your e-mail so you can check it."

We had other strong points, but we would not use all the arguments for our entire defense in this first audience. Diego would use two more points. There were more or less four points:

Two Of Diego And Two Of Mine.

This was just the beginning we could not show our entire defense. I kept the strongest point for last.

"Lawyer, do you already have what I asked for?" Diego asked me.

I had the proof of the address where Ritesh would stay. We already had an apartment, which was under my name, available for him.

Everything was perfect, and I showed them to both, Michael and Diego, to check if everything was fine. But suddenly, I saw Michael looked too serious and thoughtful like he was not convinced.

Michael just listened to us and said:

"There is something that worries me. This request for the precautionary measure differs from ninety-nine percent of what is seen in this country because this is a case of extradition, but the man is not from here. He is required by the United States. The judges may not give it to us because they may think he will escape. I always put myself in the place of the judges, you can make the attempt, but I am not very convinced."

Regarding our four strong points, he said: "You can advance something, but not much. Remember to leave the best for the last audience."

"I know, Michael", Diego told him. But those four points that we will mention will be a small detail so they know who they are dealing with, I am Diego Molina.,"

"Do you agree with this, lawyer"? And he looked at me. I answered: "Yes, lawyer, I agree one hundred percent." I looked at him seriously supporting him completely. Sometimes, lawyers need that compliment.

Michael was not very convinced, but I did, and so was Diego. If the judges denied us the precautionary measure, this first hearing would change the negative image about Ritesh and show that there were inconsistencies in the file.

We waited for the two days to receive the Ministry of Health's proofs and present the formal request to the court.

Before saying goodbye, I agreed to notify him when I received the four certificates from the Ministry of Health. After this, I left his office.

I waited two days eagerly to get those certificates. I realized that the head of regulated medicines was a serious person. After the two days, I arrived at the Ministry of Health and withdrew the four certificates. While walking towards the car, I could not believe what I was reading. The government of Panama had certified that the four drugs were not narcotics. However, Ritesh's file, which came from the United States, made them look like such and that Ritesh had, therefore, committed a narcotics trafficking conspiracy.

The fact that the Panama prosecutor did not even bother to analyze these details, or worse, that she did not have the knowledge to understand the truth saddened me.

I called Diego to share the news, we were both very excited. In the afternoon of that same day, Ritesh called me and I informed him about the four certificates, he was positive and said:

"Henry, I have little time to talk, but it's important to remind you about what I consider the judges at the Court must know". He recalled that Interpol officer who, acting as a businessman, tricked him into coming to Panama.

Then he proceeded: "We have exported these drugs legally after they were approved by the FDA India. If I had committed any fault or crime, I should have been arrested in India, since the USA government has an extradition treaty with India.

Why did they dupe me, inviting me to Panama, trapping me in a hotel and arresting me?

And so ended our conversation.

Wednesday, September 9th, 2015
Diego and I were ready. We already had our four proofs and went to court to present the request for the hearing where we would formally request the precautionary measure.

When we entered the Court, everyone greeted him, as usual.

We arrived at the Second Criminal Chamber where there were three receptionists at the entrance. One receptionist welcomed us, received the document and stamped it.

That document contained all our personal data such as our telephone numbers so they could keep in touch to tell us the day the judges would grant us the hearing.

Two days later, they called to give it to us on Monday, September 14th, 2015, at 5:00 p.m.

Ironically, there was a day left to complete the sixty days since Ritesh was arrested in Panama.

That afternoon Ritesh called me, like every afternoon, and I gave him the good news about his first hearing where we would request the precautionary measure, the house for jail. That day, he was ready for being transferred from the jail to the court. I called Vivaan, who also showed a lot of joy for the news. We were all positive and ready to face the challenge.

MONDAY, SEPTEMBER 14TH, 2015.
PANAMA, PANAMA CITY. SUPREME COURT OF JUSTICE
4:30 PM.
Diego and I had arrived at the Supreme Court thirty minutes before for any eventuality. We went in my car that day. I parked, and we both

got out of the car and headed towards the Court when Diego asked me:

"Lawyer, since you were at the control hearing, who is the chief or main magistrate?"

"The chief magistrate is Joe Cavalli," I replied.

At that moment, he closed his eyes and moved his head from one side to the other.

And I asked him: "Is there any problem, lawyer?"

And with worry he said: "That guy is a son of a bitch", while taking a deep breath.

Judge Cavalli had ten complaints about abuse of authority. He was well known at the national level. Among all the judges of the Court, he was the one who had the most complaints.

We went up to the stairs and walked to the Hearing Chamber of the Supreme Court of Justice.

When arriving at the room, the prosecutor was outside talking with the translator. Neither the judges nor Ritesh had arrived. The prosecutor told us, in an unfriendly tone, that next time we had to bring our own translator since for the first hearing the Public Ministry had contributed with it, but for the others, we had to be in charge. We didn't tell her anything because we didn't want to be distracted by the audience. So we did not follow her game.

I found out with a security agent that Ritesh had already arrived at the court. He was in the court cell, where detainees usually wait. I ran to the cell and knocked at the door, but I couldn't enter. However, they opened a space for me to see Ritesh.

Two policemen escorted him. As soon as he saw me, he stood up, handcuffed and shackled on his feet. I could tell his feelings from his eyes. He felt destroyed. I tried to encourage him by reminding our promise and commitment, but he didn't say anything. He was speechless.

I said: "Look, here we are". Diego is there waiting for me, I went to say hello and I want you to know that we are with you". He only shook his head. Then, I said: "We'll wait for you out there". And I went back to the Hearing Room.

In the courtroom, we were confirmed that the Judges had arrived and that we could take our place.

I sat next to Diego while we were waiting for Ritesh. Next to Ritesh was his translator. The prosecutor had already arrived and was sitting on the other side.

After a few minutes, the three judges entered. They sat down and took their places in the Chamber. They ordered to look for Ritesh at the court cell.

We could hear Ritesh's arrival because of the sound of the shackles dragging along the floor, a very sad scene. That's where Ritesh comes in and takes his place, next to his translator and next to us.

It was 5:10 p.m. and the Chief Magistrate, Joe Cavalli, began speaking:

"Ladies and Gentlemen, Good Afternoon". We announce the start of the hearing requested by the defendant, a request for a precautionary measure."

There is an opportunity to present both the Public Ministry and the defending party, or us.

The prosecutor gets up, tells her name and announces that she is representing the Public Ministry.

At that moment, the judge asked my name. I noticed his look of surprise for seeing such a fresh and young lawyer. His eyes sparkled with curiosity. Then, after observing his smile of admiration, I replied: "My name is Henry Lopez. I am one of Ritesh's lawyers. But I'm not the one who will speak, Mr. Judge. The principal lawyer in this Chamber is Mr. Diego Molina." I informed him.

At that moment, the prosecutor looked at Diego, and Diego introduced himself: "My name is Diego Molina and I am representing Mr. Ritesh Ambani."

But almost everyone knew Diego. He did not need a presentation.

The Judge-Rapporteur continues: "giving follow-up to the present hearing..."

At that moment, Ritesh started trembling. He said he was cold. One judge regarded him and with an exaggerated surprised face asked him if he was okay. I did not like his look. Everyone in the Court observed Ritesh, who did not stop shaking hard while saying: "It's cold, it's cold." The judge ordered to turn off the air. It was not so cold indeed, but it is obvious he was shaking with nerves.

The chief magistrate gave the opportunity to the representative of the Public Ministry of Panama through the prosecutor. She started reading two long pages and I could see that they were the same two pages that she had taken to the control hearing.

My name is Yolanda Rivera and I am the prosecutor representing the Public Prosecutor's Office. We have received the request for extradition against Mr. Ritesh Ambani from the Government of the United States through the Foreign Ministry. Ritesh Ambani is accused of the following charges:

1. Conspiracy to import non-narcotic drugs category IV.
2. Money laundering through an online pharmacy that Mr. Ritesh owes, which he operates to sell these types of medications that are not prescribed and may be forged. The four medications mentioned are Tramadol, Carisoprodol, Viagra, and Cialis.
3. Different charges for mail violation.

Among the things I was reading was narcotraffics conspiracy. It was not within the main charges for which he was required, but it appeared in the file and in the documentation that was sent to Panama. Something striking that ignites the alert of any country.

That was the end of her speech and the Magistrate Speaker gave the opportunity to Diego.

Diego, the distinguished lawyer would speak; and I would be by his side supporting him in everything. It was Ritesh's decision and as the client, it was his right to set up the conditions.

Before Diego started talking, he was interrupted by the Magistrate Speaker who said: "You only have fifteen minutes to sustain, Mr. Molina."

These are the things that you do not expect. The man has not even started talking and they are already setting time limits. It was the last audience of the day; it was already past 5:00 p.m., so the judge wanted to go home. But I disagree with it. If this happened to Diego, a respected and recognized lawyer, imagine what it would have been like for a not so well-known lawyer?

Unlike the prosecutor who brought his two long sheets, Diego had everything in his head. He had studied the last two days.

At that moment, he began by saying:

"How is it possible that an undercover agent from the United States comes to question a person in my country without the Public Prosecutor's authorization?" He had reviewed the portfolio, the documents and the laptop which is an illegal action since, according to the Code of Criminal Procedure, the only person who can approve an undercover operation is the Panama prosecutor. This agent did it without the Public Ministry's authorization.

That was one of Diego's strongest points and he said it from the start, he told me he would hit hard. He also told them how that aspect violates several articles of the Constitution of the Republic of Panama.

As he had only fifteen minutes, he did not have much time to reach out, and he told them about the four certificates of the Ministry of Health which clearly state that none of these drugs are narcotics. However, one of the charges stated in the file was narcotics conspiracy, which means traffic of narcotics, an argument for extradition that our client didn't deserve.

Ritesh was deceived by an undercover agent who made him believe he would do business in Panama. He mentioned all the articles of the constitution; he knew them by heart, as a true connoisseur.

When he finished talking, he looked at me and said: anything else?

Then, I whispered: "The four certificates evidence is missing, Dr. Read what the four certificates say"

If the prosecutor read her pages, we would also read our evidence. So, I passed Diego the four certificates provided by the Ministry of Health one by one. He began to read them.

Certificate 1
Panama, Republic of Panama
The Panama Ministry of Health, through the Department of Pharmacies and Drugs Department of Controlled Substances, certifies that the drug Tramadol is not a narcotic.
Sincerely,
The Director of Controlled Substances

Certificate 2.
Panama, Republic of Panama
The Ministry of Health of Panama through the Directorate of Pharmacies and Drugs, Department of controlled substances, certifies that the drug Carisoprodol is not a narcotic
Sincerely,
The Director of Controlled Substances.
Diego could not pronounce the word "Carisoprodol" in English and became entangled.I felt sad about this because if I had read it, it would have been another story.

Certificate 3.
Panama, Republic of Panama
The Ministry of Health of Panama through the Directorate of Pharmacies and Drugs, Department of controlled substances certifies that the drug Viagra is not a narcotic.
Sincerely,
The Director of Controlled Substances.

Certificate 4.
Panama, Republic of Panama
The Ministry of Health of Panama through the Directorate of Pharmacies and Drugs, Department of controlled substances certifies that the drug Cialis is not a narcotic
Sincerely,
The Director of Controlled Substances.

"For the foregoing, I request, gentlemen judges, mercy for this gentleman who is suffering from being detained in a cell together with extremely dangerous criminals,"

When Diego finished pronouncing the word "dangerous", I looked at one of the judges. There was one of them, who moved his face as if to say no. It was the same one who had previously looked at Ritesh to ask him if there was something wrong. I did not like this approach at all.

Diego continued: "And we can show the documents of a residence where Mr. Ambani will stay. I passed the document to him and he took it to the judges."

The main magistrate thanked Attorney Diego Molina for his participation and asked the following question:

"Madam Prosecutor, do you agree with us granting the precautionary measure house for jail to Mr. Ritesh Ambani?"

The prosecutor stood up and said: "No, I do not agree with the precautionary measure, Mr. Magistrate."

And the judge continued: "We will have a ten- minute recess to think about the subject. When we return, we will let you know our decision."

When the judges left, Diego, and I looked at each other.

Diego told me, "Your support was outstanding,"

"Do you think so?" I said.

"Unquestionably, "he replied.

The memory of the judge's face, as he shook his head kept me worried. I did not know if Diego had noticed it, but I did. And I was not convinced that they would give him the precautionary measure. I looked at Ritesh, and I saw him praying.

The translator did a good job. I listened to him constantly translating so that Ritesh could understand almost everything in that hearing.

After a few minutes, the judges entered ready to announce the decision.

"We, the Court Magistrates of the Second Criminal Court on behalf of the Republic of Panama and administrating Justice, are ready to express our decision based on the request for the precautionary measure in favor of Ritesh Ambani."

First, since the defending party mentioned four points that are not used for this type of hearing, but for the occurrence of objections or the last hearing, our decision is to deny the precautionary measure "house for jail" to Ritesh Ambani. As a result, we reaffirm the detention that he keeps and give continuity to the extradition process."

And so the judges stood up, turned around and left.

Ritesh looked at me, but he said nothing. There was a blaming look as if saying "this is your fault, not mine". I could understand that look. People always find someone to blame when there is a problem.

Ritesh stood up; the policemen put the shackles on his feet and accompanied him to the exit. After the judges, he was the first one to leave.

The next day, Ritesh called me, and told me: "There is nothing wrong, I believe in you."

That made me feel a little better.

CHAPTER 15

The Arrival of Amil and Vivaan Ambani to Panama

I RECEIVED CALLS FROM RITESH almost every day, he urgently said to me: "Get me out, get me out of here please", I answered to him: "We are working on that. Have faith."

His brother also called asking how things were going on and wishing us good luck.

Vivaan had told us that he had to settle some issues with the Panama visa, the first to arrive in Panama would be Amil, Ritesh's friend.

Apparently, in the Ministry of Foreign Affairs of India, they were told that Panama was a very dangerous country and that they should be very careful because they came to Central America, a reference that was not true because Panama is one of the safest countries in America.

The first to arrive would be Amil, who used to call me by cell and write to me by WhatsApp. As he was afraid, he had asked me to please pick him up at the airport, to which I agreed.

I remember the night I went to look for him at the airport. His arrival was at 7:30 p.m. He was coming from Newark, New York since the flight made a stop in NY. It made me happy to know that there was somebody coming from India to support Ritesh.

It was already 7:30 p.m. and Amil's flight had arrived in the country. I was just waiting for the check-up and for him to show up at the exit door. When I finally saw him, I knew it was he, first because of the

Hindu features and because he had sent me a picture so that I could recognize him.

When we finally met, we shook hands, introduced ourselves and smiled at each other.

I saw that he was a very nice and cordial person and, like Ritesh, he made that cobra head movement to show gratitude and kindness meaning that what I was saying was nice for him.

From India, he had asked me to recommend a good hotel in the center of the city, so I got him a good one.

He thanked me for picking him up at the airport. Once at the hotel, we said goodbye. It was the arrival of the first person close to Ritesh Ambani.

It was a long trip and he looked tired.

While in Panama, Amil could meet Diego, meet his office, my office and also see the things we had already done for his friend. Diego and I were already moving in the case.

A week after Amil's arrival, Vivaan had already called me and told me he had his visa ready and that he would arrive soon. He told me the date, as I had already told Amil that Panama was a quiet country, they did not feel afraid, so I did not have to go to the airport to look for him.

When Vivaan arrived in Panama, he wanted to meet me that same day, so he demanded that both Diego and I go to the hotel. I arrived at the hotel earlier than Diego, so I got to see him first.

The first day I saw Vivaan, I noticed a fixed and attentive look, like someone who distrusts, or someone who is aware of the risk taken when trusting a person one does not know well. Unlike Amil, he was the one that stood out for this detail. He shook my hand, we smiled at each other and he said: "You are young, you are younger than my brother and I and you are younger than I expected".

That same day in the afternoon, Ritesh called me from prison. His voice sounded more motivated because his people had come. Family is worth more than a thousand encouraging words.

I already knew what Ritesh would say: "Get me out of here". But Vivaan told me that this was what his brother had kept begging for since he had been sent to prison. When Diego Molina arrived, accompanied by his colleague Michael and his son, I introduced them. They all greeted one another.

For the number of people at the hotel's lobby, Vivaan asked us to please come up to his room to speak in private and we all accepted. It would have been better if we had held the meeting in the morning at Diego's office or mine, but Vivaan was very interested in meeting Diego personally and could not wait.

When we got to the room, I was still translating Diego and Vivaan's conversation.

At that moment, Vivaan asked Diego:

"How do you see my brother's case? And what possibilities do you see?"

"They have violated your brother's fundamental guarantees," he replied.

Diego spoke in Spanish so fast that he did not even give me time to translate.

He raised his voice in an imposing manner as if it were a fight. He talked about the constitution, in an altered tone, he cited the articles. Obviously, Vivaan did not understand, he only saw an altered man speaking in Spanish, a language he did not know.

Diego looked imposing and powerful. Among the things he said was: "I, Diego Molina, will do everything possible to avoid that extradition to the United States."

When Diego finished speaking, Vivaan lowered his arms together as if in adoration. He knelt on the floor and bowed several times while saying: "Now, I am happy."

I embraced Diego, and he hugged me. We all said good-bye pleasantly.

CHAPTER 16

Amil and Vivaan Visit Ritesh in Jail

EXTRADITION CASES ARE BROUGHT BY the Supreme Court of Justice of Panama and those who decide whether extradition is viable or not are the judges of the Supreme Court of Justice.

The legal process in an extradition case begins with the control hearing, which provides the detainee with knowledge about the process and his rights such as the elements required for his defense. It is basically the hearing when the detainee has knowledge that a process will be followed and that he will have all the elements to defend himself. First, it is necessary to wait sixty days for evidence from the United States to arrive.

We usually define an extradition case in the last hearing. In this hearing, Ritesh's defense would have all the time to present all the points for which we consider extradition or all objections unfeasible. We knew that the last audience was the decisive one.

We all met; Diego, Amil, Vivaan and I and we explained all this, so they had a clear picture of the process that Ritesh was going through. They asked some questions, which we were pleased to answer to guarantee their understanding and their satisfaction.

At that moment, Vivaan, told us:

"I would like to visit my brother in the cell."

"No problem", I said, I can help you with this first visit". I offered my car, and we agreed on the day of the visit. I recommended him buying all the things a day before because we needed to be there early due to the distance (the jail was two hours and thirty minutes from the city) and the process requirements.

By that time, I had already obtained permission for special visits. I had it in my hand; with this permission, Ambani's brothers could enter. In a country where they knew nothing, being able to see Ritesh was too great for them, almost unbelievable.

On our way to the cell, they spoke their language among them, so I did not understand anything.

Vivaan had bought a lot of packaged food from India to take it to his brother. There was a kind of packaged chicken, with curry of the same brand.

When we passed all the controls, the moment of truth finally arrived.

Upon my arrival, I requested Ritesh, who joined us in a few minutes. The meeting was filled with sad scenes. When they saw each other, they broke into tears, especially Ritesh. They talked for almost two hours, but Ritesh could not stop crying. His tears rolled down his cheeks like the stream of a mighty river. Then, I confirmed that there are people with feelings and values, but above all, that the sincere love of brothers reflects the greatness of a family. This is the saddest meeting I have ever witnessed, but at the same time, the most inspiring one.

When the custody chief announced that the visit period was over, they said goodbye with a trace of sadness in their eyes.

Ritesh said: "Thank you, Henry; I have no words to thank for what you are doing for me." He looked at me and I saw gratitude in his eyes. Then, Vivaan said: "What you are doing is from God and it is very important. We need to be back in India for our children are waiting for us."

Vivaan walked towards me to tell something in private: "Henry, I'm very grateful for everything you've done for me and my brother. I will always remember this and I will always thank you."

To which I replied: "Thank you for trusting us." At that moment, he embraced me and I felt he was sincere.

We were in a secluded place and two hours from Panama City. I was the eyes of these people in Panama. He continued saying: "Henry, we will be doing several errands in the city, we will ask for help from the consulate of India in Panama so that Diego and you can concentrate on your work."

"It's okay," I said.

CHAPTER 17

The Form and the Fund

DIEGO, MICHAEL AND I PREPARED our defense.

Being gathered in the office, Diego made a comment: "We were fine, but this will not be easy."

There's a lot of time left for the final hearing, but from now on we can call Peter."

Peter Rodriguez was considered the only extradition specialist in the country. Even though he had had only three, he was considered then one with the greatest number of extradition cases.

Diego proceeded: "I've thought about him since the beginning because I knew about this case. I had him in mind."

At that moment Michael shook his head as if in denial and said: "I do not think that's a very good idea."

"Why do you say it?" asked Diego.

"Of all the extradition cases that he has seen, I do not know of a case that he has won, I think he has lost all of them," he replied.

"But the guy has seen more cases than anyone; therefore, he must know a lot about them," Diego insisted.

Michael, being older, had witnessed old cases of national and international level, but Peter had lost all of them. In fact, Michael had a lot of experience; his hair all white convinced anyone. And if there were two people who knew about his great potential and intelligence were Diego and I.

In life, there are very intelligent people who stand out from others and Michael is one of them. Many people respected him for his humbleness because he did not care about material things. Most of his clients were poor people looking for a solution to their problems.

Panama is a small country where there have been few cases of extradition in relation to other large countries of the first world. Perhaps, this is why there was only one specialist in extradition cases. As this case was with the United States, Michael asked his daughter if she knew of a lawyer in the United States specialist in extradition cases and who had won at least one case. His daughter found one. Michael sent him the file and we focused on "THE FORM" of the case. All this would be presented at the last hearing.

An extradition case is divided into two parts: **THE FORM AND THE FUND**

The form is all the elements that the extradition request must have.

A request for extradition may contain an error in the file preparation if it does not fulfill the law requirements.

Title IX of the Third Book of the Penal Code of Panama in its article 521 states: The request for extradition must be made before the Ministry of Foreign Affairs through the respective diplomatic agent or, in the absence of this, by his consular agent or that of a friendly nation, accompanied by the following documents:

1. In the case of a person who has been convicted, a copy of the final judgment, the evidence on which the request is based on and a statement of the fact that the sentence applies and the degree to which the sentence must still be met.
2. In the case of an accused, a copy of the arrest warrant and the order for prosecution or pre trial detention, and the evidence on which the decision is based.
3. A precise statement of the facts making up the imputed offense, when they do not appear in the documents stated in the preceding paragraphs, which describe the acts or omissions that make up a said offense, a sign of the time and place of their commission and participation of the person required.

4. The legal provisions that establish the jurisdiction of the requesting State and the definition of the offense, and the norms regarding the prescription of criminal action and punishment.
5. Special data that allow establishing the identity, nationality, and location of the person claimed.
6. In cases where the death penalty applies, a decision of non-execution of the sentence.

These are the main aspects of how the extradition request should be made. There are others, but these are the most important ones. If any of these points are not expressed properly, the request for extradition fails.

The Fund, on the other hand, is the offense, infraction or crime committed, which has to be proven. In this case, the sale of medicines.

Both Diego and Michael were clear that I was the specialist in the subject of narcotics, non-narcotics, and medicines in general, in the issue of imports and exports.

Basically, I had absolute control of the subject, but having complete mastery of the fund doesn't guarantee winning an extradition case. Although it seems incredible, my background was not enough because what the judges evaluate the most is the form. There is no better way to convince the judges than supporting both, the form and the fund.

What Michael, Diego and I were planning was hitting with the fund and destroying them with the form. I was part of a team of winners. Diego even told me: "You look like me, only younger." "Two great dreamers with a positive mind,"

Every day we found something new in the file which did not treat any other subject, except this. I was thoroughly focused on this case, committed to finishing what I had started and to never give up: the key to achieving anything in life.

One day, early in the morning, I went to the Supreme Court to request the last thirty extradition files. With these last thirty cases of extradition, I locked myself in my office to read them and study them one by one. I focused on that for two weeks.

Despite the true that the chances of winning an extradition case are very remote because of its complexity, I was determined to win. I put the twenty-nine lost cases aside, and the case won apart from them. But, I didn't neglect the lost cases. After a complete analysis, I realized that some of them had even made a good defense. I saw defense points that seemed to be right, so I considered each one.

Sometimes there was nothing to do. They were lost cases because the crime was proven, but the lawyers took advantage of some oversights in the file's form to accomplish their goal.

As I read more and more about the extradition law, I discovered more about the mistakes made by the lawyers. During those two weeks, there were nights when I did not even sleep at home since I was reading and looking for more information.

The interesting thing is that the extradition cases are public by law. The Government of Panama has to publish them in the newspapers. The names of those requested for extradition and their crimes also appeared on the internet with their respective dates.

It was very interesting, to have a file, to put the name of those requested for extradition and to see that they appear in the news when doing the search in Google.

We knew that everything would be resolved in the objection incident, better known as the last hearing. In Ritesh's file, I had already pointed out twenty-two violations or points in favor of Ritesh. Not counting those found by Diego and Michael.

But of all of them, I had discovered a powerful one. It was about giving shape to that point, I do not know if it was true and it had to be confirmed with a legal basis.

It was 3:17 a.m. when I finally tied all the ideas and had the basis for this new point.

I was so happy that I wanted to call Diego and Michael right away, but obviously, they were both sleeping. So I wrote all my ideas and waited impatiently to call them and give them the good news.

It consisted of attacking the main charge that was held, I mean: conspiracy to import controlled substances from List IV. I communicated it first to Diego at 9:30 a.m. with an awesome joy.

I did not call him before because I had to call Pharmacies and Drugs in Panama at 9:00 A.M.

"Doctor, how is it going?"

"I found a very strong aspect in our favor.

Listen to me very well and pay attention.

In the main position: Conspiracy to import controlled substances from List IV

Ritesh was not an importer. Ritesh was an exporter from India. The importer was the person who bought him the medicines. This could be proved with the migratory movement of entry and exit since Ritesh had not even entered the United States. The exporter is never responsible neither in Panama nor in the United States.

I already consulted with the Ministry of Health of Panama, Department of Pharmacies and Drugs and they confirmed that no exporter has been convicted in Panama, only the importer."

And the extradition treaty between Panama and the United States says that for it to be extradition it must be a crime both in Panama and in the United States."

Diego answered: "Excellent, we already have them, but we will leave this point for the last audience." Do not mention it yet, this is our strongest point together with that of the narcotics. Tell Ambani's brother to request the migratory movement in India."

I mentioned all the points I found. In the file, there was a website that was supposed to be Ambani's, but when I joined the site, I discovered it belonged to an Australian Furniture. The file had many contradictions and mistakes that we could take advantage of.

After calling Diego, I was curious to know the requirements considered by the US entity to approve an extradition case, so I contacted the entity by phone to find it out by myself. Fortunately, I could talk to the director who confirmed what I suspected.

I did not give him names or details of the case, but after greeting him and identifying myself, I stated the question: "Is it possible to approve an extradition case when the one involved is an importer instead of an exporter?" It is not considered a crime in Panama, and for an extradition case to take place, we must categorize it as a crime in both, Panama and the United States. Also, drug trafficking conspiracy is one of the charges in the file, but none of the drugs turns out to be narcotics.

I had not even finished saying the word narcotics when he lost his temper. He had a rough reaction and hung the phone. In fact, he did not answer my questions. He said some words harshly, but I could not understand, because he got tangled when speaking.

I did not tell Diego, but I had found another new point in the file and it was a way out before the last hearing. If he succeeded, Ritesh could leave without having to go to the last audience. I did not tell him because I had to keep investigating this aspect.

Several of the lawyers in the twenty-nine cases I read had spoken about the evidence within sixty days.

CHAPTER 18

The Proofs Within Sixty Days

ARTICLE 525 OF THE EXTRADITION law between Panama and the United States establishes that the request for provisional detention must be accompanied by the formal promise of the requesting State to present the request for extradition within sixty days, counted from detention of the person required. This is known as the proofs within sixty days.

Ritesh had been arrested on July 15th; the sixty days would be fulfilled on September 15th.

I went to the court to verify if the proofs had arrived, but the secretary told me that they hadn't, which meant that if in five days the proofs did not arrive, they had to release Ritesh.

I left the Court laughing, like a great calculator just waiting for the moment to strike, but I had mentioned nothing to Diego. Almost every day, I received a call from Ritesh or his brother. This happens in these cases. I think that if you let yourself be influenced by this pressure, you can make mistakes.

I started counting the days on the calendar, the days that were considered business days. There were no vacations for those days, so the deadline was Friday, September 15th. I was even more involved in the case than Michael and Diego, but they were also doing a good job. Deep down, I also wanted to take the credit.

As we were under the new accusatory penal system, everything had to be supported in the audience. So, I prepared the letter with all the arguments and with the request for a hearing for formal support.

The days were long. Everything went through my mind. For example, if these proofs would come. It was five days, but it looked like ten.

I called foreign relations in Panama; I wanted to go to them to verify this. They told me they did not attend the public, and that I had to follow up from the court. They also did not want to give me information by phone. Then it was clear that the evidence had to be in court because if they had reached foreign relations they would have sent it immediately.

I knew that I could not go to the court every day to ask because I would alert them, and I could harm the case. I had only one thing: to arrive at the court on September 15th and ask if they had received the evidence, and if not, submit the writing. If they had arrived, there would be nothing to do.

I had Ritesh's voice in my mind: "Get me out of here". I had not told Michael or Diego about my plan. I wanted to give the blow because I felt there was something strange about the proofs, why had not they reached the court? Why hadn't we seen them?

Why did the Ministry of Relations, extradition department tell me they did not serve the public? In the court, I was told that the proofs had arrived; however, when requesting them, they did not have them.

It was September 15th; I went to the court at 2:00 p.m. I acted with caution; I would only leave them three hours ahead, I was sure that they could not move with these proofs in three hours.

I entered the courtroom, and I talked to the secretary.

"Hello, how are you? Did the evidence for Ritesh's case come?"

She replied: Yes, those proofs came."

I told her: May I see them?"

And she answered: "Yes, it's okay."

She searched everywhere and began making calls anxiously.

At the end, she told me that the proofs had not arrived.

Then I shouted: "Good!"

I will present the following writing.

She read it, but she told me that I could not present the document because those proofs would arrive soon, only that they had been delayed.

Then I said: "I would like to present it, it does not matter if they arrive or not". She made calls again, this time she was more nervous than before.

It's amazing how a kingdom behaves. Even the secretary was on behalf of all of them and against an innocent detainee.

Suddenly, the main secretary of the three judges entered. The one that is only seen in the audience next to them. She shook her head and allowed me to receive the document.

Finally, the secretary at the reception received it.

Why wait for the last hearing if I could finish all this here?

I could do this because, with the power of attorney that we had presented at the Court, I was the second lawyer in the case, so I had the right to do it and I did it flawlessly.

Diego was also doing a good job, but I was devoted to this case. I love what I do and when you have so much passion you feel unstoppable, and you feel that eventually, you will get what you want.

It is possible that the calls from Ritesh and from his brother where they asked me to take him out of prison finally made their effect. Everything was already done; we just had to wait for the Court hearing to expose the subject of the evidence within sixty days. I made a mistake because I had to consult Diego, but deeply inside I wanted to surprise him.

It was a perilous move. If we won, they released Ritesh. If we lost, nothing would happen; there was still the last audience. I knew the magnitude of the situation.

Being at my house that same day at 7:30 p.m., I received a call from Diego. I did not know anything about him in several days, but that day he called me.

"I saw what you did, you damaged the case. Do you hear me? I never told you to do that, why did you do it without consulting me. I have a contact that tells me everything that happens in court. That's why I found out."

Diego was furious. "You already damaged everything", he told me again.

Diego found out because he sent his assistant that day to verify that everything was fine, and his assistant, saw the file and the letter, requested a copy of it and took it to Diego.

Indeed, Diego did not have any contact in court; he carried out the case honestly. Without contacts, without corruption. But as he is known by everybody, it was easy for him to make me believe what he stated.

He would not let me speak in the telephone conversation, he was extremely upset, and that's when I said: "Diego let me explain."

Then he heard me.

"Diego, I got thirty files of thirty cases of extradition from the court, twenty-nine lost and only one won. Some lawyers used all the files and the subject of the evidence within sixty days."

Diego understood my point. And I said again: "Dr. the proofs have not reached the Court, the secretary got nervous and started making calls.

Dr., you can verify that the evidence is not in court. Please read article 525 of the extradition law that talks about the evidence."

And he says:" Wait, I have the code here, let me read it", and after reading it, he understood me.

"I think you're right. We grabbed them," he said, eagerly.

And I told him: the best thing is that we still have the last audience if we lose this one.

I found this alternative as a great option for not reaching the last audience. But Diego told me that they could take the day sixty-one as a valid day yet.

When the sixty-one arrived, Diego went to the court at 4 p.m. and stayed there until 5:00, but the proofs didn't arrive. At the court reception, he told both the secretary of the reception and those who were present:

"Five minutes to five o'clock in the afternoon and I, Diego Molina, came to check that these proofs never came."

Diego and I felt satisfied; Diego just hoped that they would give us the audience to support.

On Monday of the following week, we were both notified for the hearing

Diego told me: "Leave everything to me that I take care of it."

I told him:" It's fine."

I gave him only one recommendation. In the last hearing, the prosecutor brought a couple of long sheets and read everything. This does not mean that we would do the same, but it was important to take notes of the most relevant things about the case and read them. He agreed on that.

Besides the second one, Ritesh Ambani would have a third audience. I called Vivaan to tell him the good news, and he told his brother.

We were ready for the audience. Ritesh called me that same day in the afternoon, and I told him about the hearing, I told him that he would be taken to court.

I explained to him what this hearing represented and that it had been created by us, it was not in the script, that is, the only obligatory audience was the incident of objections better known as the last hearing. I explained that this would be a great opportunity that we would have without having to reach the last audience, and he understood it.

CHAPTER 19

The Movements of
Vivaan in Panama

MEANWHILE, VIVAAN AND HIS FRIEND were almost every day stuck in the
Indian Consulate in Panama. In the consulate, they already knew them
and their case as well.

They were told that they would send letters to the Panamanian government in support, letters that were never received. In fact, the consulate never supported them in anything. They were not interested in
understanding the file; they were not interested in anything.

The consulate had a relationship with the Hindu community established in Panama for many years. They were introduced to the President
of the Hindu community in Panama and Vivaan wanted him to meet
Diego and me.

Diego and I explained the case to him. When I spoke, I watched his
face of admiration.

However, after he left the office I did not see him anymore, and I
think he didn't do anything else.

The president of the Hindu community did not lift a finger, but he
asked Vivaan how much Diego and I had been paid.

Sometimes I did not understand why Vivaan went so much to the
consulate, for me it was a waste of time. There are consulates in Latin
America that strongly support detainees outside their countries. The
consulate of Ecuador in Panama, through its humanitarian action,

supports them unconditionally, including Panamanian lawyers at their disposal.

I felt that what the Indian consulate in Panama did to Ritesh was to ignore him and run away. They turned their backs on one of their own people when he needed it most. But Ritesh survived in that place because of his intelligence.

Ritesh had a lot of problems in jail. He did not have clothes and Vivaan asked me to help him with the permits to bring clothes and more food to jail. It was packaged food, mostly chicken since he did not eat beef or pork. I got him the clothes and all the permits.

Amil, Ritesh's friend, took many pictures of Panama; he had never been to our country. He was not anguished as Vivaan, he was calmer. Vivaan was in charge of everything, Ritesh was not alone.

CHAPTER 20

The Hearing of the Proofs Within Sixty Days

THE DAY OF THE HEARING arrived. Amil had met a fellow countryman at a Hindu restaurant and befriended him. He was a Hindu – Venezuelan with scars from a burglar shot attack in Venezuela. He offered to take Amil and Vivaan to the court.

The audience was programmed for four in the afternoon, but Diego and I had agreed to meet at 3:00 p.m. just in case of any unexpected situations.

We were ready. The central theme of the hearing was that the evidence did not arrive within the sixty days established by law. There was no other topic to be discussed at that hearing because the judges would say that any other issue had to be addressed during the objection or final hearing incident.

Because of the request of the Public Ministry Prosecutor, we got our own translator. The one in charge of translating all the documents in our firm was a young Panamanian girl who was also a lawyer. She asked me to pick her up to go to the court together, and I agreed.

We arrived at 3:00 p.m. and Diego was already there. We greeted each other for several seconds. It was an embrace of respect confirming that we were together in this and that we strongly supported each other.

We were a few meters from the audience room. Thirty minutes later, we saw them approach. Vivaan, Amil and Amil's new friend. They greeted us with a hug and got into the room one by one. There was also Diego's son and all his office staff. He had given them the day off because he wanted them to witness his audiences. (They always do it)

Unlike the previous audience, Ritesh was not alone. He was with his people.

Diego had his entire defense and arguments prepared. Closing his eyes, he whispered some words as if giving himself more motivation. I tried not to distract him, so I introduced the translator and let them talk for a few minutes. At that moment, I went to greet and encourage Ritesh by telling him about the presence of his family, which caused him great joy.

I quickly returned to where Diego and the translator were. By then, almost everyone had entered the room. I asked Diego if we could enter together, and he requested me to advance because he needed to stay a few more minutes tuning some details for his speech. So I agreed and I went with Paola, the translator.

When Paola and I got to the room, it was almost full. In fact, there were even several television channels from the outside providing coverage.

Upon entering the room, our presence was remarkable. I could say that I had taken care of all the audience's details. For example, I had given Diego all my analysis on the sixty days five days before. In addition, he added much more content that he considered necessary.

On the other hand, I had not neglected any detail of my personal image. My hair was properly fixed and I was wearing my best black suit, which gave me a touch of peerless elegance and neatness. I looked very handsome, and so did the translator.

Being captured by the local media made me feel very important. I was not nervous at all. On the contrary, I felt very safe. Indeed, an inexplicable feeling embraced my soul when the cameras from outside caught our entrance. I felt like a new soccer player in the big leagues!

Both the translator and I took our seats and prepared to wait. Only the three judges, Diego Molina, and Ritesh Ambani were to enter the courtroom.

Aftera few minutes, the three judges appeared and took their respective seats. Upon arrival; the judges ordered a policeman to bring Ritesh Ambani, leaving the courtroom door open so that he could enter. Meanwhile, when Diego realized it, he entered the court.

It was not until that moment that I understood why he wanted to enter last. When everyone was in the room, Diego went directly to the three judges and shook hands with everyone.

A few minutes later, we heard the shackles on the floor announcing Ritesh's arrival. But this time, it was another Ritesh. Walking with his head up and looking calm and enthusiastic, mainly because of the presence of family and friends.

Upon entering, we heard Ritesh relatives' voice; He looked at them and told them that everything was okay. He sat next to us; we greeted one another.

Soon after everyone was in the room, the judge rapporteur began the hearing:

"Ladies and gentlemen, we, the magistrates of the Supreme Court of Justice on behalf of the Republic of Panama, consider Mr. Ritesh Ambani's hearing to have begun today."

"First, we will give the opportunity to the Public Ministry."

At that moment, the prosecutor began to make her disclaimers.

The prosecutor took out her long sheets as in the previous hearings and started reading them, but I noticed that this time, she had three more sheets.

She started by reading the first two charges: Conspiracy to import non-narcotics category IV and money laundering, but for the audience's surprise, there were twelve more charges found later and added to the file.

Diego and I looked at each other wondering why. If Ritesh had already been called at the Control hearing on two counts, how comes there were more charges against him?

The prosecutor read all the charges, which were mostly charges for mail violation. Being accused of fourteen charges, everything looked so complicated for Ritesh.

Once the prosecutor finished reading the documentation arrived from the United States, the magistrate rapporteur gave the opportunity to the defense of Ritesh, so Diego started:

-Dear Magistrates and Public in General

We will begin our defense by invoking the constitutional guarantees of Ritesh Ambani, which have been violated. The government of the United States has sixty days to send the evidence, as it corresponds to Article 325 of the Criminal Procedure Code that says: Article 525 of the extradition law between Panama and the United States provides that the request for provisional detention must be accompanied by the formal promise of the Requesting State to submit the extradition request within sixty days, counted from arrest of the requested person. This is known as the proofs within sixty days.

September 15th, 2015, was the last day for the United States government to present the evidence; we gave it one more day, which was September 16. On September 16th, I stayed from 4 p.m. to 5:00 p.m. in the Supreme Court of Justice, where there was no entry of the mentioned proofs. They never arrived.

We have all the stamps of entry of the documentation that we presented and the stamps of entry of the documents by the United States with the exact hours. As stated in the documentation that I am submitting.

And he began to read the exact hours of entry of the documents and the exact time where we presented our resource.

"Besides, you all have to know that Ritesh Ambani was tricked into coming to Panama. An undercover police officer checked his wallet, his cell phone, and all his belongings, a measure that only the prosecutor in Panama can carry out. Nobody may conduct undercover operations within our country without the prosecutor's authorization.

Drug trafficking conspiracy appears in the file referring to drug trafficking as narcotics trafficking. However, none of the four drugs are narcotics.

I was impressed by his majestic voice. My skin bristled at how skillfully he was leading the audience. Diego also mentioned that no other charge could be added, except those for which the defendant had initially been brought to trial.

He mentioned three strong points besides the sixty-day tests.

Diego's intervention was outstanding. When he finished, he put away the microphone and said to me in a low voice: "I was born for this. This is the love of my life. I will die in court."

When Diego had finished speaking, the judge rapporteur began his speech. Then, something unexpected happened.

Ritesh asked for the microphone to speak before the judges.

Diego looked at me and mumbled: What is he going to do now?

I was more than surprised. The judges were amazed, the head judge asked: "Do you want to talk Mr. Ritesh?"

And Ritesh said: "Yes, I want to speak, Judge"

What is he going to talk about? Diego whispered again as if begging him to shut up.

At that moment the main judge looked at Diego and said with a face of concern and amazement:

Lawyer, Diego Molina: "Did you know that your client, Mr. Ritesh Ambani, wanted to talk?"

Diego could not hide his concern, his gaze was clear. "No, Judge, I didn't know", he replied. The judge, still in astonishment asked: "Attorney Diego Molina, do you agree that your client speaks? "Diego Molina looked up as if wishing our client changed his mind. However, he answered: "It is ok, Mr. Judge". Let my representative speak.

Diego and I could not hide our worry when we passed the microphone to Ritesh and he started talking. Ritesh very confidently and calmly said:

"Ladies and gentlemen, I was tricked into coming to Panama to do business. An agent from the United States who made me come to Panama deceived me. If India has an extradition treaty with the United States, why did not they request my extradition in India? I have all the licenses to sell medicines granted by the FDA of India, or the Ministry of Health. I never left India to do business in the United States."

Gentlemen Judges, My future is in your hands"

Diego touched Ritesh's legs to stop him because anything could be used against him.

Both Diego and I were very concerned with his intervention until he finally fell silent.

Analyzing everything he said, I did not feel there was anything wrong with his words, but Diego was not happy at all. In addition, this hearing was to speak about the sixty days of the evidence. In the last hearing, we could talk about everything else.

Once Ritesh was silent, the magistrate spoke again and asked the Public Prosecutor's Office represented in this case by the prosecutor Yolanda Rivera: "Do you agree to give Mr. Ritesh liberty due to what was pointed out by attorney Diego Molina"?

The prosecutor energetically answered: "No, Judge, I do not agree." But she did not explain why.

At this point, the main judge announced a recess for the three judges to deliberate the decision. When everyone got up, Ritesh's relatives approached him. I felt as positive as Diego regarding our first attempt.

At the end of the recess, the judges entered one by one. The chief judge gave his verdict.

"The evidence within sixty days arrived in Panama within the term because they reached Panama's foreign relations within sixty days. It is true that the evidence was not sent from the foreign relations offices to the Court in the term, but it is not an error from the United States, since they sent it within the limit. If the proofs had not reached Foreign Relations, then we would be talking about something else, and the defending party would be right.

So we deny the request for liberty based on the evidence of sixty days and order sixty days of arrest from today. With this, we declare the hearing adjourned"

Ritesh lowered his head in a sign of discontent. He did not even look at Diego, but he approached me and said with a hint of sadness and hopelessness. "He is not a powerful lawyer?"

My response was: "Yes, he is. Diego is famous in Panama." However, his feeling was natural and unavoidable. He felt defeated and so did his relatives, who expected us to accomplish his freedom.

The judges left the court and the three policemen, who were guarding Ritesh, helped him get up and put his handcuffs and shackles back.

At that moment, we heard the heartbreaking cry of Ritesh's brother, Vivaan. Ritesh breathed deeply as if taking strength and told his people that he was fine.

We all came down from the Court. For me, it had been a hard blow. My face reflected my dissatisfaction and I still wondered why we hadn't been successful. But Diego's son was even more affected. He got frustrated to see his father lose.

When Ritesh left the room, Diego approached him outraged and said in a serious and exalted voice that we all heard:

"I was doing my job. Why did you have to talk? You sank yourself with your own mouth". At that moment, the translator intervenes. Ritesh did not answer anything. The poor man was already too distressed.

We stayed for at least fifteen minutes at the exit door of the court trying to understand what had happened. Diego asked the translator to accompany him because he had some words for Vivaan.

"Ambani, are you satisfied with the service we have given you?", Diego asked.

The translator translated and Vivaan Ambani responded: "One feels satisfied depending on the results." to which Diego replied: "your brother did not have to talk; the fish dies by its mouth."

Faced with that loss, Diego felt that Ritesh should not have spoken, but he also explained his feelings about what the judge decided.

"How could we know that the document had arrived at the Foreign Relations Extradition Department? When I called, they told me that they did not have an office for the public. They suggested me going to the court to find it out by myself. I am being honest. This is what they told me. Things like this only happen in a third world country.

For me, Diego was a hero, I hugged him and said: "You are an extra-dition lawyer. You are the best, you have my respect."

After that audience, Diego will always have my respect. Besides, it had been my mistake. He supported me and stood in front like the big ones, so I had promised myself to support him, too.

I left the court accompanied by the translator. While I was driving, I could not think of anything else. My mind was in blank. I felt the urgent need to express my disappointment.

"I think I'd better withdraw from the case, "I told Paola

She immediately replied: "Vivian Ambani's response to Diego was incredible. When I heard that answer, I was stunned. My God, what a response!"

I insisted on my position: "I confess to you, Paola, I'm well beaten. I think I will withdraw from the

case. Instead of getting him out with the argument of the sixty days of the proofs, the judge told

us about sixty days more in prison. This is unbelievable!!!

Paola tried to encourage me by saying:" God will give you the wisdom for this case."

Once at home, I pondered about the case to get things clear, but it was difficult for me to understand and accept the unexpected outcome. The judge's words echoed in my mind, but I think they brought Ritesh an echo from the depth of his soul.

Unfortunately, this is one of my country's weaknesses. In Foreign Affairs, the department that has to do with extradition cases, they did not attend me upon the excuse that it is not for public attention. By that time, it was the law. I do not know if nowadays things have changed.

In other words, we had no way to know if the proofs had arrived. It remained a mystery. I also wondered why the Court secretary was so nervous that day when I requested the proofs.

But, of one thing I was convinced. Diego had directed a tremendous audience. Everyone in the room witnessed it, and I am sure that everyone would agree that it was a good attempt we had to feel proud of.

However, Diego was not calm. His pride was hurt, so he wanted to appeal to the right of habeas corpus. I supported him, but I kept thinking about the last audience. While the habeas corpus provides the opportunity to discuss the illegality of the detention, the final hearing is the decisive one, where a good lawyer gives the final thrust.

The next day, I received a call from Vivaan. He wanted to meet with me, so we agreed on the time and day to see each other. At the meeting, he told me: "Henry, I want you to continue in the case, my brother has asked me. You cannot leave us now, I know you're affected, but please, don't give up"

I was not affected. I was, extremely affected.

"Henry, no lawyer handles as much knowledge of my brother's case as you, and no one who arrives just now will handle as much information as you do. You look a little bit sad, please do not leave, and do not leave my brother alone"

What I perceived from Vivian's attitude was fear. He was afraid that his lawyers would give up the case. It seemed they still had faith in us. I admit that the mistake had been mine because I was the creator of this audience over sixty days, not Diego. But, he was convinced this argument was enough to request his freedom.

Ritesh Ambani had to be released that day, if international laws are not respected, I did not want to be part of that, and I thought that day to retire from being a lawyer

Trying to analyze everything Vivaan said, I answered: "Do not worry, be calm, you are the ones who rule and I will stay with you, I will not leave." and that's how our meeting ended.

My analysis of the case took a week, during which I talked just a little with Diego. After that, I asked him to meet and he accepted. When we met, I said: "You did very well, you have my respect". Honestly, I did not do it to cheer him up, although he needed it, but because I put myself in his place.

And he said: "Thank you, Henry." Then, staring at me, he told me: "Henry, in the last audience I would like you to be the one to expose, you know more than anyone else about all this, so this is your case, Henry. I will be by your side accompanying you"

I could notice in his words he had already overcome the blow. His words came from the heart. He already had a plan, to proceed with the Habeas Corpus and to let me lead the last hearing, which was, in fact, my desire from the very beginning.

From that moment, I understood that we were both undefeatable warriors fighting together for the same cause. But, most important, we were loyal to each other. In my country, loyalty is highly valued. Being the main lawyer who would speak before the judges gave me more self-confidence, and having Diego next to me provided me more reassurance.

I knew we had sixty days to prepare for the final hearing. Again I had to go back to the books, and re-read the extradition cases, but this time, I came up with a different alternative. As Albert Einstein once said, do not expect things to change if you always do the same. I knew it was time for a different strategy.

I had thirty files, twenty-nine about lost cases and one that had been successful. This time, I did not read any of the twenty-nine. Instead, I opened the one that won, dated 2002. It had been many years since that case. I looked for the name of the lawyer who had won it. By that time, he was a seventy-five-year-old man who had already retired from law. He was a famous lawyer, too.

I managed to find the phone number of the firm he worked for and luckily, I got his home number. Alberto García was his name.

RITESH'S WIFE

After this lost hearing, something momentous happened. Ritesh's wife began a strong internet campaign that lasted several weeks. She was requesting his husband's freedom, ensuring his innocence and the legality of his business since he had all the required licenses to act as an exporter. Using the argument about India's extradition treaty, she wrote to all the highest authorities asking for support.

It was an incredible demonstration of devotion, a sincere opening of her soul. I could perceive her willingness and powerful, unconditional love for her husband. Eventually, she stopped writing, which I interpreted as resignation.

CHAPTER 21

Alberto García, The Retired Lawyer Who Won an Extradition Case

I CALLED DIEGO AND EXPLAINED what I had in mind; I wanted to meet with the only lawyer of the thirty files I requested that had won an extradition case.

I asked him to go with me because it was quite important, to which Diego agreed. Diego knew him and told me it would be a pleasure to go. At that time, Michael was having high blood pressure problems, so he could not accompany us.

When I told Diego the lawyer's name he told me: "I won a case against Alberto, he knows who I am. I am Diego Molina."

I chuckled a little bit, but Diego didn't notice it. I thought for a moment: Diego is a good lawyer, but sometimes he brags a lot about it. Actually, Diego is proud of his accomplishments and he does not like to be compared with another lawyer, even though this other is older than he.

The day of the meeting arrived. Don Alberto Garcia had given us his homeaddress. I arrived a little earlier than Diego so that I could talk to him a few minutes before getting started.

To describe the house, it would be enough to say that it was practically a mansion, built at the end of the nineties. It looked kind of old, but beautiful.

When I arrived, I introduce myself and so did he.

"Dr. Alberto, it's a pleasure to meet you, I've read about you."

"The pleasure is mine, Henry. So …you have an extradition case?" He told me with a suspicious tone. "Oh, son! You're too young to get into something so serious. Do you know how many extradition cases I saw and how many I won? I only won one and I saw three in all my life. That's very hard to win, Henry."

I asked him: "Don Alberto, do you know Diego Molina?"

"Hahaha!! Diego is an artist! I know him." He is well known, he understands the essence of what a criminal lawyer is. Besides, he is a clever guy. The media is always looking for him and that's what he loves the most".

Then, with a mischievous look, he added: I also fell in love with fame. It let me enjoy a luxurious life I didn't want to get rid of. I loved it to such an extent that I would have killed and died for it. Indeed, it was my true love. I was always chasing it like a mad man and when I had it, it turned into a sickly vice until the moment I had to face my retirement. In other words, fame changed my life.

"Seeing Diego is like seeing myself in a mirror several years ago."

When the doorbell rang, we knew it was Diego.

Upon entering, Diego raised his arms once, to embrace him.

"It's a great pleasure to see you again". "Allow me to hug you with all my respect, Don Alberto."

"The pleasure is mine Diego, says Don Alberto," you are an artist, Diego!"

"And you are a legend, Don Alberto," Diego answered.

To describe that moment, it was a very respectful hug. They acted like two friends who had not seen each other for a long time.

Up to that moment, I had not told Don Alberto about my idea. My plan was to make him part of the team. But, Diego was already there, so I started explaining what I had in mind.

"Look, Don Alberto, my idea is to add you to the group and make a super powerful team.

"I am the one who speaks at the last hearing, but I need lawyer number two and number three behind me, your presence in court and if it is possible, even in the public."

At that moment, he looked at me and Diego and said: "It's okay, Henry; it's an honor that you have chosen me as part of the team, I can support you, but what I do not want is to handle the case in the media because I'm already retired. I can read the file and see all the errors made during the process"

"It seems good, Dr. Diego and I would be in charge of the media", I said very pleasantly.

This was what we needed; now we could have a true specialist acting in the process.

In the faculties of law of the universities in several countries there are professors of Private International Law, but how many of them have seen an extradition case? None! The true teacher in this matter is the one who has won an extradition case in court, and this one was, without any doubts, an expertise.

I got him updated about what had happened in the court. "We just lost an audience on the subject of the sixty days of the proofs, what do you think about that?"

"Never trust the sixty days hearing, nobody wins at the sixty days hearing. The case that I won, I went to the objection incident or the last hearing." he told us.

I tried to explain that we were not in the control hearing. We took the case later, and in our first hearing, Diego and I requested the precautionary measure of house for jail.

"We presented all the evidence, including that we had got a place where Ritesh Ambani was going to stay and the judges denied us that precautionary measure. Don Alberto, why do you think the judges denied us this hearing?"

"Simple, Henry. For the risk of flight," he answered.

Diego and I looked at each other and we remembered Michael, who had told us the same. But the hearing was not bad because it helped us to make ourselves noticeable and send a message of several irregularities found during the process.

Being a small country of only four million people, where there have been few cases of extradition, where very few lawyers have won, we were with the lawyer who best understood this issue throughout the entire country.

When I read all the last thirty cases, I saw that there is a group of five lawyers who even repeat the cases. Always the same, nobody understands this better than these five. Without any doubt, this gentleman represented power for us.

I continued saying: "Don Alberto, I have over fifteen strong points and Diego has ten strong points. But of all my points, I have two lethal ones."

In the file, the USA government talks about narcotraffic conspiracy. As you know narcotraffic is narcotics trafficking. We have four certificates issued by the Ministry of Health where it says that none of the four is a narcotic.

He approached me and, with a look of great respect, said: I love this point, but do you know where this point is going? Take out the extradition law between the United States and Panama and read article 533:

They are grounds for extradition objections.

Item 4. "That the request for extradition is contrary to the law or of any treaty to which the Republic of Panama is a party."

Diego and I looked at each other in surprise. I was super excited when I added: "But I have another one which is even more lethal", and I told him everything.

"Bring me the file Henry, I will read it and look for all the points and contradictions.

That boy is ours! They will give it to us, right Diego?

Diego looked at me and replied: "I already told Henry that Ritesh will not live in the United States. He will stay here in Panama. Hahaha!!!Both laughed.

I had read and studied the extradition process many times. I thought I already knew everything about it, but there was an article that I did not know. I was with Diego, one of the best in the country. We had Michael and now we had Don Alberto. We all understood the language of the judges.

I felt unstoppable. I kept thinking about that final audience for many weeks, but it wasn't merely for money. I felt like a prisoner struggling for freedom. Furthermore, I knew that winning this case would open the door that would lead me to gain the credibility required for further cases of extradition.

Diego looked silent and quiet as if he were plotting something else.

"What's the matter, Diego?" I asked him.

He looked at me with a deep and determined look and said:

"What happens is that my son got frustrated after the last hearing. I will enter Habeas Corpus.

And I replied: "Ok, but remember that it will be defined in the last hearing".

I did not agree with the Habeas Corpus, so I asked Diego to please not do it. When I asked Don Alberto about his opinion, he didn't answer immediately, but about three hours later, he gave me his answer behind Diego's back.

Once the meeting was over, we said goodbye and left the house of the retired lawyer, Don Alberto.

It was 7:00 p.m. and I was already at home when I received a call. It was Don Alberto.

"Hello Henry, I need to talk to you about something important", he said

"Tell me, Don Alberto".

"I do not agree to present the Habeas Corpus, but I did not dare to say it in order not to hurt Diego. You're right, even the points you have are much stronger than his points and I like them more. In fact, I did not win my case with Habeas Corpus. I won it in the last hearing."

As you know, Habeas Corpus will not stop the last hearing, but... Listen, Henry: Diego will enter that Habeas Corpus and neither you nor anyone can stop him, you'll see."

"I understand Don Alberto. Diego also knows that this is defined in the last audience, but there is something else in this: Pride and honor. I saw it in his eyes and I think he is doing everything possible for that man to stay in Panama."

And as it was expected, Diego presented the Habeas Corpus. This time he did it by himself. He didn't use any of my strong points.

On the other hand, Amil Ritesh's friend had to leave Panama; he had commitments in his country. The only one who stayed was Vivaan.

CHAPTER 22

The Narcotics Agreements
for Extradition Issues

THAT NIGHT AFTER THAT MEETING with Alberto García and Diego, I was super motivated. I was at my house analyzing many things. For instance, I remembered what Michael told me one day: "You are young and you had never seen an extradition case, but you master this specific case as a true specialist. Besides, there is no one specializing in extradition, so you are the best to defend it together with Diego and me. Not even in Costa Rica, Panama or throughout Central America will you find a lawyer who understands this as you do. It must be the reason you are so devoted to the case."

Those words from Michael gave me a lot of motivation. How something so simple, could be complicated? How did they dare to put in that file that Ritesh was an importer and that what he was interested in was narcotics?

The narcotics agreements for extradition issues was to combat drug trafficking. To be more clear, the trafficking of cocaine, heroin or marijuana. They were not created to fight against a medication to treat generic pain, which made them see that they were apparently false. The proof is that on the list of these agreements did not appear any of the four drugs sold by Ritesh.

But the question is: How did they see that he was an importer?

I was sure he was innocent. If he was extradited, it was going to be cruel and unfair.

I turned on my laptop to find more information on the subject and to know what was happening in the United States. I found a lot of information, and so I could understand many other aspects:

The information I read from the newspapers was:

NEW DELHI - India, the second-largest exporter of over-the-counter and prescription drugs to the United States, is under increasing scrutiny by US regulators for lapses in security, falsification of drug test results and sale of fake medicines.

India's pharmaceutical industry supplies forty percent of the over-the-counter and generic prescription drugs consumed in the United States, so the increased scrutiny could have profound implications for American consumers.

"If I have to follow United States standards to inspect the facilities that supply the Indian market --said the chief drug regulator of India, in a recent interview with an Indian newspaper,-- we will have to close almost all of those facilities."

India's pharmaceutical industry is one of the most important economic engines in the country, exporting fifteen billion dollars in products every year. Some of its factories are world-class, practically indistinguishable from their Western counterparts. But others suffer serious problems of quality control. The World Health Organization estimated that one out of every five drugs manufactured in India is false. A 2010 survey of New Delhi pharmacies found that twelve percent of the drugs in the sample were fake.

And I kept finding more about the international operation against the sale of illicit medicines on the internet. A hundred countries have taken part in a global operation to dismantle criminal networks dedicated to the illicit sale of drugs over the Internet, which has led to the arrest of fifty-eight people worldwide and the seizure of nine million dangerous drugs, valued in about forty-one million USD.

In Operation PANGEA VI, the largest worldwide operation carried out to date against illicit websites dedicated to the online sale of fake or low-quality medicines, has involved police and customs services and national regulatory bodies, which besides acting against websites selling counterfeit and illicit medicines, have promoted an awareness of the serious health risk that can be caused by the purchase of medicines on the web.

This was a great international movement, a social health problem. I also put myself in the place of those people who are buying these fake medications, and who do not have FDA approval. It can be risky for their lives.

The pharmaceutical industry supplies forty percent of the medicines consumed in India, so this operation is nothing against India, it is against a small group of people doing things illegally.

That night, I went to bed at four in the morning and ended up understanding much more of the situation. I understood that even if Ritesh had done something wrong, he had already paid for it, he even told me one day that if that business brought problems to his life he did not want to know more about it.

Being on the other side also allows you to see many things, the human side of people, their tears, their suffering, and the misfortunes of their lives. Ritesh was not a bad person and although, as a drug connoisseur, he knew that the ones he sold were harmless because they did not represent any danger to humans, other medicines that have been confiscated from other Indian exporters have been dangerous drugs for cancer, diabetes, and other complex diseases.

CHAPTER 23

New Changes

TWO WEEKS AFTER THE HEARING, Vivaan called Diego to hold a meeting. The reason for the meeting was that Vivaan wanted to know Diego's defense plan to free his brother from then on.

He asked me to please talk to Diego to make an appointment. At that precise moment, Diego was preparing for another audience, another very famous one that was taking place in the country. All the national media gave coverage to that case.

I tried to explain this to the Ambanis:

"Vivaan, Diego is a prestigious lawyer, and he is currently seeing another very important case that is coming out in the media almost every day. Remember we have to wait sixty days, and then your brother's audience will come. Give Diego two weeks to get him out of this hearing and go back to your brother's case.

And his response was: "He has forgotten my brother for being in other cases."

I tried to explain to him that Diego had already requested the Habeas Corpus and that we were waiting for its admission.

Vivaan had stayed in Panama for at least three months to visit his brother and share with him.

There was something very important that I felt I had to tell Vivaan, and I was ready to tell him, not knowing that this would change the fate of his brother's case.

"Vivaan, as you know I am a specialist in the subjects of medicines and narcotics and in the matter of imports and exports. Consequently, Diego wants me to be the one who speaks at the last hearing. But I also need you to know that we have incorporated a new lawyer, one who won the only case of extradition that has emerged victorious in the country. He will support by investigating the documents' arrival. He is an expert in these cases and we would add the points of Diego, and mine. You need someone to get up and say: Wait, "I sold these medications, so I can show you my knowledge on the subject."

His answer was very confident and with a friendly smile: "I prefer it to be Diego or someone of Diego's age, you are too young Henry". At that moment, he patted my shoulder and said goodbye.

I understood that I would not speak at the last hearing.

It was necessary to wait for the sixty days of detention decreed by the judges, but now Ritesh's freedom depended on the final hearing and the Habeas Corpus that Diego had entered, whose admission had not been granted yet.

A month passed, and I knew nothing about Vivaan until he called me one day for another meeting.

The fact that he did not write or call me for a month seemed strange to me.

I attended him in my office that day and without Diego. I noticed a smile as if he had good news followed by an enthusiastic greeting: "How are you, Henry?" to which I replied with the same enthusiasm.

He looked very safe, and he continued saying: "Look, Henry, I have many things to tell you. To begin with, I need to meet Diego, but some-times it's complicated. How is it possible that you cannot meet with your lawyer? I think communication is something essential. Do you keep in touch with him? Do you see him often?"

I tried to defend Diego by reminding him that Diego was attending a great case and was preparing for the audience.

After the sixty-day hearing, I had more respect for Diego. For me, he was a warrior, but not for them. They got stuck in the lost audience and someone had to take responsibility. Who was the perfect target? The lawyer who presented it. I even felt that for them, Diego was more responsible than I, which wasn't really true.

And he continued saying: "In addition, we had bad results. The results have not been favorable, Henry, so I moved for a month.

I took advantage of the situation to make it clear: "The person responsible for the sixty-day audience is me, not Diego", I admitted emphatically.

He continued saying: "I've talked to a lot of lawyers, you cannot imagine how many."

I felt betrayal in his eyes, which made me very sad. I do not know if because I looked very young, but I noticed a somehow haughty and superior attitude. And he said: "Henry, the day you have contact with the judges, the day you buy the judges to win the cases; that day you will make a lot of money."

At all-time he kept laughing and sure about what he was saying. But, I still did not understand anything, so I asked him the question. "Then, you have a new lawyer, don't you?"

He shook his head affirmatively: "We have found a new lawyer and I want you to meet with him and give me your opinion."

I did not understand why he wanted my opinion. But I was curious to find out who the new lawyer was, so I asked him: "And what is the name of the new lawyer?" Deep inside I knew this question was unnecessary; it was more a matter of curiosity.

And he said: "The lawyer's name is Mauro Lombardo"

I knew who he was and, to be honest, I did not like him very much. He liked to show off; he was a man of over sixty years with dark skin.

"I know who he is," I said.

"Do you know him? He asked with admiration." And is he a bad or a good lawyer?"

My response was honest to him: "I do not know, I have not heard from him for years, and I do not know how many cases he has won or how many he has lost. As a result, I cannot tell you whether he is good or bad."

And he replied: I will have a meeting with him in his office tomorrow. I would like you to go and give me your opinion."

"Ok, I'll be there," I promised.

I called Diego to tell him what happened, and he asked me:

"Lawyer, are you going to that meeting? That is humiliating"

"Yes, I will. I will do it for Ritesh. No problem, but I am a little curious"

When the meeting arrived the next day, I headed according to the address that Vivaan had given me. The office was in a residential area. It was not in a building like mine or in a commercial area.

Upon arriving, I saw Vivaan standing on the sidewalk, beckoning that this was the place. I parked my car and headed towards the meeting room, which the receptionist had shown me.

Two dark-skinned lawyers were sitting in the boardroom. But neither of them was Mauro Lombardo. I introduced myself, and the meeting began. This was like a betrayal. At that moment, one of them named Daniel looked at me and said:

"Lawyer, can you give us your impressions of the case, and tell us how things are going on?"

My response was almost immediate, "I will make a brief summary of the case." Thus, I told them

the whole story since Ritesh was arrested by an undercover agent in Panama. At that moment, he looked at me and said: "Can you give me the copies of the file?"

When asking this question, I saw Vivaan. I found the answer on his facial expression; little by little, I understood what was happening. But the strange thing is that I didn't know them and I did not even remember having crossed them in any court. Also, if the copies could be obtained from the Court, why did I have to give them to him? I only asked two questions, and the first was:

"Can you both tell me your full names?"

And they both told me their names.

As extradition cases are public, all the lawyers who have taken extradition cases in Panama appear in the online newspapers. Even if they have won or lost the case. Of course, the vast majority has lost them. Right there, sitting in the meeting room with them in front, and while the meeting was taking place, I took out my cell phone and I put their name on Google along with the word extradition.

Neither of them appeared as lawyers having dealt with extradition cases before, not even when I typed Mauro Lombardo's name. Google is a wonder where you can investigate anything, even a person's life.

I asked them the second question: "Have you ever seen an extradition case?"

One of them looked at me with confidence and answered: "Yes, we have seen."

"I asked you this because we took this clients from the third day he was been detained in Panama. We have a job done, we handle the extradition language. We have studied thirty cases of extradition. We already have experience on this, which has allowed us to handle the extradition process. And to be honest, it would be very sad if the whole case falls down."

Then, he replied sarcastically: "If the client comes to us, it is because he feels dissatisfied with the work you have done so far. Now, excuse us, but we need to talk to our client."

And the last thing he said was really a humiliation. He practically kicked me out of his office. While the other lawyers continued talking, I kept silent, just thinking about what Vivaan had decided. I really did not understand why he had invited me to that meeting if he had already chosen other lawyers.

Besides, it was a matter of loyalty. Diego and I had already started together, we had to continue together. And if this new group of lawyers wanted me alone and not Diego, I was not going to participate. Now, the issue was that they did not want either of us.

The first thing I did as soon as I left was to call Diego and tell him everything about the meeting.

And Diego told me: "I congratulate you, Henry. You deserve all my admiration and respect; you showed love for your client. The Ambanis will see the difference. Those lawyers are going to use our ideas"

I continued complaining: "And now that we have strengthened our power with Dr. Alberto, now that we have such a powerful and peerless team, we are going to be displaced by these new lawyers who lack both, experience and good intentions." "I think they will crash sooner than expected"

To all this Diego responded: "The one that will crash is Ambani."

In an energetic tone, Diego told me: "I'll give you a piece of advice, lawyer: Get out of that case. Listen to what I say. "Do not go against the grain. God is taking us out of this case. They made their decision and that will not change."

"Ok, lawyer," I replied.

"Henry, you found the truth, we were close, we could have made history, and even Michael told me so."

I wanted to know about that new lawyer and I asked Diego: "Dr, one last question, do you know those three lawyers? The two I met and their boss, Mauro Lombardo? What can you tell me about them?"

And he replied: Ha, ha, ha! Of course! I know Mauro Lombardo very well, I know his intellectual capacity, but he is not at your level, you are more intelligent than he.

I could not think of anything else, I was focused and, without realizing it, I had become a specialist in extradition cases.

The next day, Vivaan called me. He wanted us to meet again.

Why did he want a new meeting now? I did not understand anything. He did not even call Diego. It was only with me. We agreed to meet in my office, I attended the meeting punctually.

CHAPTER 24

The Contact with the Judges

I THINK HE FELT HE had to give me an explanation, so at that meeting, he started saying: "Look, Henry, I wanted to team up with you and the new lawyers, I asked my new lawyer, but he told me that he could solve this problem without Diego and without you."

Wao! I said in my mind: This is a killer; this is the man who will give classes to Diego and me about how things are done.

"Ok, it's fine," I said.

Then, he proceeded: "I'll explain a little: Do you remember when I told you that I had been looking for lawyers for a month? I asked many if anyone had contact with the judges. "Well, I finally found a good lawyer. The new lawyer told me that he has contact with the judges and that my brother will be freed. Moreover, my new lawyer told me that my brother would leave with the same Habeas Corpus that Diego had entered and that everything was ready, so we are just waiting for that. I do not know if it's true or false. But I do not have another option, Henry.

I understood why Diego did not want to be part of these things and he told me to stay away. When Vivaan said "my lawyer", I did not know with what intention he did it, whether he did it naturally or on purpose because his lawyers were Diego and I.

Upon hearing all this from Vivaan, I thought: "Either for good or for bad, Vivaan looks so confident, that he is taking for granted his brother's freedom".

Then, he continued saying: "Look, I liked this country and I've seen a lot of business that can be done here. We would make money very easily, like this "- He snapped his fingers.

"I already talked with my brother and when he leaves prison, we will stay in Panama to do business."

He was so sure that his brother wasn't going to leave Panama that he had even made plans for their future.

"Look, Henry, I just want to ask you another question. Do you think they have contact with the judges?"

I thought a bit about the answer because I really did not know. Apart from the fact that his lawyer was also known in the country, so I limited myself to say: Do you remember when I asked them at the meeting if they had seen any extradition case? They said yes, but after my research, I discovered they do not appear to have seen any case. So, they lied."

Vivaan bowed his head as a sign of sadness.

I restated: "I cannot tell you if they have the contact or not because I do not know.

Besides, what makes us different is that we guarantee a clean defense. I have no idea about the method they plan to use, but if they are lying, they are playing with your brother's life. ".

I felt with the authority to warn him about the imminent danger to which he was exposing his brother: "Your brother is smart. That's why he chose us. But now, you found this new lawyer and you are free to do whatever you want, but what you are doing is to goes against your brother's will and against what we have done for him, so far."

Nevertheless, my warning didn't cause any reaction. Quite the opposite, he gave me a sharp answer: "Look, Henry, I have to go to India; otherwise, I lose my job. I have to leave. Amil has already left Panama for work issues. He stayed here only for a month. My new lawyer will be in charge of the case, whatever I need, I'll call you. I appreciate your support.

At that moment, Vivaan said goodbye to me and I did not know more about him and the case.

I called Don Alberto Garcia, Diego and Michael to tell them we were no longer in the case, that they had hired another lawyer, but I never gave the details of what Vivaan told me.

Either Vivaan had taken control of everything or his brother had given him complete control.

I remember that one day, when I visited Ritesh in prison; he told me he was smarter than his brother. I feel that Ritesh had lost credibility in his own capacity and potential.

The story of Ritesh's defense was being completely changed by his brother. His story would take another direction by a new plan we would not be part of.

CHAPTER 25

One Year Later

A CALL FROM INDIA

It HAD BEEN A YEAR since Ambani had been arrested. Even though I was still working and seeing other cases, I always remembered him, but I had followed Diego's advice to get away from that. Although I admit that it had hurt to leave.

Most people, when faced with something difficult, tend to surrender. For instance, most lawyers who heard that it was an extradition case against the government of the United States considered it a lost cause. It was like David against Goliath. But, I have a different point of view about life challenges. I think that nothing is impossible if you have it in your heart and you believe and work hard for it.

One day, I received an unexpected call from India. It was Vivaan.

"Henry, how are you?"

"Very well, thank you and you?" I answered

Well... thank you, he replied with a hint of sadness.

"Next week, I will be in Panama. My brother is still in custody because the judges have not answered Diego's Habeas Corpus yet. I do not know why it has taken so long. The lawyers promised to release him, but time goes by and nothing has happened so far. Could you go to court to see how things are going on, please?"

The extradition process takes between four and six months, it takes more time if the lawyer takes legal actions such as Habeas Corpus. In other words, what had held Ritesh in Panama at the moment was Diego's Habeas Corpus.

In order not to be impolite, I accepted to go. I was not following Diego's advice, but deep inside I was curious to see how everything was going on. Besides, there was a special feeling for Ritesh. So, that same week I went to court to see if there was something new, but I felt really surprised to see that everything remained as Diego and I had left it. No other lawyer had entered any document. In other words, Diego and I maintained ourselves as the lawyers without even knowing because the other lawyers had not even entered their power of attorney to represent the defendant. They hadn't formalized anything yet.

Regarding the Habeas Corpus, it was still in process without even a date for ratification.

All this seemed strange to me that the new lawyers have not entered the power of attorney.

I did not know it. From court, I called Michael to update him.

And he said: "Lawyer, they have not done and will not do anything. They are making a lobby."

This means reaching an objective through a dishonest or not transparent way.

The next day, I called Vivaan to tell him about it, but he did not say anything at all.

It felt like when a person is clinging to something he wants to be true. In his mind, he wanted to believe that everything was correct and that the new lawyers really had the required contacts and the guts to be victorious. Anyway, I told him that and I had kept disconnected from that case for several months.

I realized that Vivaan was the one who had handled everything. He had his style of directing, he had his own ideas and his own thoughts.

CHAPTER 26

I Have No Answers
From My Lawyer

ONE YEAR AND THREE MONTHS of Ritesh's detention had passed, when I got a WhatsApp message from Vivaan.

"Hi, Henry, how are you?"

"Very well," I replied.

If there is a trait that the Indians have is that they are very respectful, and they always greet you politely.

"Henry, I'm writing to you because I do not know anything about my brother's case. My lawyer only makes promises, but it is always the same story. My brother does not come out of prison, and I do not know what to do. You're the only person who tells me the truth. Can you go back to court to see what is going on?"

I understood the purpose of his compliments, but once more I accepted.

"Ok, I'll be through this during the week and I'll let you know."

Although I was not dealing with his brother's case any longer, when he requested me to go to court, I felt the necessity to help them. Besides, it did not cost me anything because I took advantage since I had to go there to see other cases.

To my surprise, Diego's power of attorney was still there. The new lawyers had not entered any power of attorney and The Habeas Corpus had not yet been resolved. I didn't have a good feeling about it.

I let Vivaan know about it. That afternoon, when I arrived at my house I told my wife everything about it. I felt satisfied because I did tell him the truth.

"Look, Regina, I went to court and there is no power of Ambani's new lawyer, the Habeas Corpus has not been answered yet, so nothing has happened so far."

It saddened me that Ritesh Ambani's case had not been solved. I promised Viviaan I would visit his brother on Friday.

This time, I wanted to know about him not as a client, but as a person. I appreciated him, and I felt grateful for the opportunity he gave me.

MY WIFE ENCOURAGED ME TO VISIT HIM.

After so long, Ritesh could not even imagine that the young lawyer who met him since he arrived in Panama would look forward to see him.

When arriving at the prison, I noticed that many things had changed. They had transferred him to another prison of recent construction but very near to the old one. The name of this new prison is Mega Jewel, much more modern one with more security controls. However, some detainees told me they were suffering even more.

I missed visiting him. I knew that his new lawyer had never visited him even though he had been with the case for more than a year. After I went through the five controls, I got to the place with the company of a custodian.

And suddenly Ritesh Ambani was coming. We greeted each other; I had not finished the greeting when he was already saying: "Tell me about my case. Help me, Henry, and get me out of here."

My lawyer always says that I will leave soon, but nothing has happened so far.

Seeing each other was a great joy. We both smiled. He was very happy to see me.

Unlike the last time, he looked very thin. His words did not match what his brother had told me. His words confused me because apparently, his lawyer was not doing anything.

"I'm in hell, Henry, this is hell." Sometimes I play dominos with the boys; I have friends here in hell.

I'm thin, right Henry? He asked me

You're pretty thin, "I replied.

The Ritesh that I met, was much more different from the one I was seeing right now.

He looked much thinner than before. He says: "You know that the worst problem here is the food, I do not eat beef or pork. Only chicken and fish."

My answer was: "Yes, I know, Ritesh. Keep positive. You are very intelligent, and you know what I mean. And I said in a lower voice: You know that you are more intelligent than all these people here, don't you?"

And he said: "Henry, there are smart people here, too."

We continued talking among bursts of laughter, but suddenly his awareness came up again:

"I know why I'm here, Henry, I did a lot of wrong things and I'm paying for what I did."

At that moment, the custodian announced that the visit was over and I said goodbye to Ritesh Ambani. But nothing could be done. Vivaan had already made his decision.

Ritesh, without a telephone and with many difficulties, had transferred to his brother all the control of his case and his defense.

That afternoon, I came to my house and told my wife everything. I had the feeling that things were not going well between Ritesh and his new lawyer, so I wanted to help him.

The next day, I received a call from an unknown number on my cell phone. It was Ritesh and he told me:

"I'm already tired, if I have to go to the United States, I will go. Can you withdraw the Habeas Corpus along with Diego."?

"Ok, well, I'll do it," I said.

I was ready to call Diego to desist from Habeas Corpus in court, but before calling him, I called Vivaan to tell him what we would do.

At that moment Vivaan told me: "Henry, do not remove the Habeas Corpus, let me consult with the family here and with a group of people to see what decision we can take together."

I could not give up the Habeas Corpus. Vivaan never called me to confirm what the decision had been. I spent two days thinking about Ritesh's plight, and I felt sorry for everything he was suffering.

AFTER BEING PAID FOR MY JOB

It called my attention that he was wearing one of the T-shirts I had bought for him. In fact, I had supported him with certain goods because he was alone in this country. Even though it is not a lawyer's job, I did it because of humanity. I also got the required permission to let him receive Indian food, specially his favorite one, chicken. I also got the permission to let his brother visit him. Getting these permissions was not an easy task and they required the approval of the Director of the Penitentiary System.

CHAPTER 27

One Year and Eleven
Months After the Arrest

I HAD A GOOD LIFE, a lovely family and a good business, too.

One day, I got another WhatsApp message from Vivaan who wrote from India.

Ritesh is still detained in Panama, but Diego's Habeas Corpus has not been answered after one year and eleven months since his arrest.

"Can you check the status of the Habeas Corpus?

I agreed to do it.

"Ok, Henry, thank you very much. I need a last favor. The public prosecutor of Panama told my brother that the time he has been detained in that country counts for two in the United States, that is, the two years he has in Panama are worth four in the United States."

"Whaaat? This news was like a bucket of cold water.

And I said: "Is your brother going to be extradited?"

He told me: "Yes, he will be extradited. In the Indian embassy, they told me that the extradition order was signed since December 2015, but my brother will be extradited in July 2017, that is, next month, when he turns two years of prison in Panama."

What a shame to hear that and my response was: "This week I will try to talk to the prosecutor"

I was so stupefied with the bad news that I organized everything to go to The International Affairs Prosecution the next day, a place I had not visited in two years. When I arrived at the prosecutor's office, which was located in the same place, a small two-floor building, I noticed everything was quite simple, nothing fancy.

When I went up to the second floor, two people assisted me: Two lawyers, the prosecutor's assistants. I asked them about Prosecutor Yolanda Rivera and they told me that she was not working there and that the new prosecutor was not there either.

Many things had changed, they even had another prosecutor. I knew nothing about these changes. They asked me what the case was, and I told them: "This is the case of Ritesh Ambani."

I asked them if Ritesh's extradition had been signed since December 2015. They told me that this was not true. The Habeas Corpus had not yet been resolved, so the information that Vivaan told me was not true.

At that moment, the young assistant attorney of the prosecutor told me:

"They did not object within the fifteen days set for objections. In other words, they did not file the petition to attend the last hearing. The Habeas Corpus was denied, and we are only waiting for the order to proceed with the extradition."

I could not believe what I heard. They made a call to the Ministry of Foreign Affairs, extradition department to confirm this information with a lawyer named Marta.

They contacted Marta and put her on the speaker. We introduced each other.

Marta said: "I am going to look for the file to give you the accurate information.

Lawyer Lopez: The defense of Ritesh Ambani did not request the final hearing and the resolution says that his defense had not shown opposition to the case. Besides, the Habeas Corpus had been answered and denied, and it was only a matter of waiting for the final paperwork to culminate with the extradition."

She gave me the resolution number and the exact date of everything.

I had to vent, and I ventured to the prosecution: "The brother hired a new lawyer after we lost the sixty-day hearing."

A lawyer should not comment on his defense to the prosecutor, but everything was lost and I began to tell them everything. My words came from my soul.

"The lawyer Diego Molina and I had the case of Ambani from the third day he arrived in Panama. He was our client. Ritesh's brother called me three days ago to know a little about the case."

In the file, the medications he used to sell appear as narcotics labeling it as narcotics conspiracy, but none of the fourth medications are narcotics.

Are you going to extradite an innocent person? " I asked emphatically.

I told them everything, even all our defense. They were listening attentively.

"An exporter detained in Panama?" An exporter had never been detained in Panama because it is not the corresponding jurisdiction. For it to be extradition, it must be a crime both in Panama and in the USA. We could not show them the conversation via email between the undercover agent and Ritesh where there is a lot of evidence in his favor.

And why didn't they capture him in India? Another questions that is still waiting for an answer.

Ritesh did not have the main or the most important audience where he could defend himself.

He was detained for a year and 11 months and had no defense because the new lawyers who took the case during one year and nine months did nothing. Neither Diego nor I were directing this. It was his brother.

When I finished, I left the office and just as I closed the door, tears rolled down my face.

THURSDAY, JUNE 29th, 2016

I called Vivaan and told him:

"I went to the prosecutor's office of international affairs and I confirmed you today that Ritesh Ambani's defense never requested the final hearing and the January resolution says that Ritesh Ambani's defense did not show opposition to the case- They didn't ask for the last hearing."

This opposition was supposed to take place within fifteen days after the young representative went to prison to take the document for him to sign, but it wasn't done due to ignorance in the extradition process or for not investigating the document that your brother had to sign.

There was a sepulchral silence while I spoke to him. Some minutes later, Vivaan told me: "A young woman went to prison and brought a document for my brother to sign, we called my lawyer and he told us not to sign anything."

I continued saying: "That document that she took to your brother, was for you to present within fifteen days the request for the last hearing. And they never did it."

He continued saying: "And according to you, which are the available options?"

"There's nothing left to do," I said.

Oh! He again told me: "Ok, I made bad decisions and because of them my brother is suffering." "What can I do now, Henry?"

I did not understand why he asked me if, in the end, he was the person who made the decisions.

"As I said before, you will not follow my opinion. You asked me for advice but you always end up doing what you consider as it has happened previously. It seems you are the lawyer, not me.

You cannot do anything in Panama now. The fight is in the United States. But I think that if I give you my advice for the United States, you will not follow it either. You will do what you think is the most convenient."

I was really upset, but I couldn't stop guiding him: "There are many things in this file that can be fought in the United States such as that it is not a narcotic conspiracy, and that he is not an importer among many other faults. I will send everything we found to your e-mail."

In a much calmer tone, he replied: "The point is that I do not want a long process for my brother, I do not want him to spend more years in jail. I think the best decision is that my brother accepts his guilt and that way they give him fewer years and he leaves faster."

Ritesh Ambani was extradited to the United States two years, two months and six days after his arrest in Panama.

He was presented to the judge in the United States, one day after his extradition. Six months later, he was sentenced to two years and nine months in prison in the United States.

According to information presented at the Court, Ritesh sent drugs from India to resellers in the United States for distribution, without a prescription to American consumers.

Monday, July 2nd, 2018
ONLY THIRTEEN DAYS BEFORE THE THREE YEARS OF AMBANI'S DETENTION IN PANAMA.

We were in the middle of the World Cup and my country Panama, which for the first time was in a World Cup, had already been eliminated. His best player, the offensive midfielder who drives the ball, was injured in the last friendly match before the World Cup.

At that moment, I got a message in WhatsApp. It was Vivaan Ambani and he told me

I would like to inform you that my brother has been released and deported to India.

We would like to thank you for the help you gave me during my stay in Panama. Thanks again for everything you did for us. This entire message was accompanied by a picture of his brother, who looked even thinner than the last time I saw him. When I saw his picture and every detail of it, I started crying. I was really excited.

My response was: "Oh, Vivaan, I am very happy for this great news.

And he replied: "Yes, I know Henry. He is finally back.

"The best news of all, thank God. Yes, we have fought for many years and finally he is out."

"I am very grateful for everything you did," he replied.

"Give this news to Diego"

"OK, I will do it."

"Thank you again, Henry," and he put the icon of two hands praying. I called my wife, I was very excited and she said something spectacular: "Good, What a good surprise!

The departure of Ambani is a good omen that we will do better"

I wrote to my mother and she was very happy.

Then I called Diego and we talked for more than an hour. I hadn't had time to talk to him, he said: "We have to sit down for lunch"

"It was an honor for me to work with you, it was an experience I will never forget," I said.

"Thanks for the friendship. The honor was mine, a young lawyer, it was very positive; we achieved important and good things in that case, thank you for the trust you had in me, I love you, Henry. " "I love you, Diego, it was my answer".

In the last three years. Operation Pangea VII, the collaboration of Interpol responsible for combating online drug trafficking, has managed to curb the illegal sales of prescription drugs virtually in more than one hundred and eleven countries, thousands of packages containing illegal prescription drugs were seized in post offices around the world, and almost two thousand websites that facilitated sales have been exposed.

The FDA stopped or confiscated five hundred and eighty-three packages in the USA as part of Operation Pangea VII. These seizures occurred in the mail centers of Los Angeles, New York, and Chicago.

The FDA also notified Internet service providers, domain name registrars and other related organizations of the 1,919 websites they found that they were selling products in violation of US law.

Operation Pangea VII led to the seizure of nineteen thousand six hundred and eighteen packages containing counterfeit or unapproved drugs sent from developing countries such as India, China, Mexico, Malaysia, Singapore, Laos, and Taiwan. The products were also shipped from more western countries such as Australia, New Zealand, and the United Kingdom. Among the confiscated products were drugs such as insulin, estrogen, and HGH, among other illegal purchases.

Many Americans apply for drugs online under the assumption that they will be the same as those approved in the US. The US, only at a lower price. Usually, this is not the case. Although the website alleged that the medication is identical to the version of EE. UU. It is an unauthorized or falsified alternative. Many illegal online pharmacies use sophisticated website templates and empty warranties to convince US consumers that the cheap drugs they sell are exactly the same as those prescribed in the US. UU

Fentanyl is at the center of the opiate crisis in the United States. It is used as a direct substitute for heroin, but it is fifty times more potent than heroin. Fentanyl is a synthetic opioid which means that it requires the manufacture of chemical precursors and is prescribed as a pain medication. In the last two years, however, the illicit manufacture and importation of Fentanyl have skyrocketed. The mortality rates due to the consumption of synthetic drugs reflect this trend.

China is the number one supplier of Fentanyl in the United States. China is also the main supplier for Canada and Mexico. The cartels usually smuggle it to the United States. After years of persistent efforts, bilateral US repression US-China on opiate trafficking has begun to have recent success. In mid-October, two Chinese citizens were accused of running a large distribution network of illicit Fentanyl and their three American accomplices were arrested.

Fentanyl exported from China to the United States comes in several forms: Fentanyl, its chemical precursors, Fentanyl variants and counterfeit prescription opiates with Fentanyl. India exports many controlled and prescribed medicines to the United States, including Fentanyl. Exports of Indian Fentanyl to the United States are a fraction of those of China, but India exports Tramadol, which is a growing problem for the United States. However, unlike China, which has now designated more than a hundred variants of Fentanyl and precursors on its list of controlled substances, India has not placed Fentanyl, or most other opioids, on its list of controlled substances, which facilitates production and export. India regulates only seventeen of the twenty-four basic chemical precursors for Fentanyl (as contained in the 1988 United Nations Convention against Drugs).

In the Middle East and Africa, the less potent opioid, Tramadol, not Fentanyl, handles the opiate crisis. India is the largest supplier.

Saturday, January 26, 2019

It was ten in the morning and an idea came up. How I didn't think about that before?

I called Diego to tell him about this: "Dr. How are you?"

"Very good, Henry and how about you?"

"Well, thank you, Diego."

"Let me ask you a question"

"Yes, Henry", he answered.

"Do you remember about the proofs of the sixty days hearing? The judge told you that the proofs didn't arrive at the court, but did they come to the Ministry of Foreign Relations? Did you see these proofs?"

"No, I never saw them, Henry."

"I never saw them, either. If the United States did not follow that case in Panama, someone from the United States never came to represent in the Court. A year later, I saw the file in court but I never saw that evidence. I still think about that. I think they played with us Diego," I said.

"What a good memory you have, Henry and yes… they played with us," he replied.

"Henry, those judges have a high level of evilness. But everything that is done here is paid. That is called karma. Why do you think the magistrates of that Court are all dying? Some get cancer, others have a heart attack for different reasons, but they all die little by little. All employees at the court know it"

Then, he told me about something that might seem taken from a horror tale.

Henry, I will tell you about an unsolved mystery in that court that seems to be unbelievable. There's a woman that appears on that place, a woman dressed in blue. One afternoon, I had a homicide hearing. You know that those audiences are long. I went down for a coffee and when I went up I saw a woman whom I talked to, but she did not answer to me. I swear to you by my mother who is dead."

"Wao," I said. "Did you see that woman's face?" No, she was on her back and dressed in blue."

"I believe you," I said.

"That woman appears in court, all those who work there know about that place curse.

But, as far as you are concerned, continue working hard. What you did was bigger than we thought. Do not stop, Henry.

THE END

ABOUT THE AUTHOR.

The author is not only a lawyer with experience in international cases but a modern bard, who is committed to his daily task. Facing a scenario that has never been imagined and without carrying a fetish, he got involved with the character of this real story living and testifying how injustice took the diabolical appearance of justice and without asking for permission to reality, closes the doors to freedom and opens the windows to dehumanization, to the little appreciation of life and the non-recognition of universal human rights. The author lived and perceived and made real the promise to write one day those real experiences within a chaotic society, deranged and vile which is inherited without turning back. The author cried, laughed and lived in his own flesh the pain of others and the indiscriminate impotence hidden in the International Treaties and in a kind of common servility done as usual. This story is for everybody who can look in that mirror, see the same scenario, live the same circumstances, and be in the same position. Only someone who has such a big heart can understand how the author struggled because heaven was his limit, and with that, he left something clear: We are not all equal, although we are all made in the image and likeness of God all-powerful.

Benito A. Mojica A. (Diego Molina's Real Name)

BIBLIOGRAPHY

Harris, G. (Feb. 14, 2014) Medicines Made in India Set Off Safety Worries. New York Times
Recuperado de https://www.nytimes.com/2014/02/15/world/asia/medicines-made-in-india-set-off-safety-worries.html

(27 de junio de 2013) Operación internacional contra la venta de medicamentos ilícitos por Internet. Interpol
Recuperado de https://www.interpol.int/es/Noticias-y-acontecimientos/Noticias/2013/Operacion-internacional-contra-la-venta-de-medicamentos-ilicitos-por-Internet

Farivar, M. (April 27, 2018) 4 Chinese Charged in Fentanyl Trafficking Case. Voa News
Recuperado de: https://www.voanews.com/usa/4-chinese-charged-fentanyl-trafficking-case

Arcia, J. (16 de marzo de 2016) Las medicinas genéricas son tan eficaces como las originales. La Estrella de Panamá.
Recuperado de: http://laestrella.com.pa/panama/nacional/medicinas-genericas-eficaces-como-originales/23928166

La Ley 75 de 1904, que aprobó la convención de extradición entre Panamá y Los Estados Unidos de Norteamérica.
Título IX del Libro tercero del Código Penal de Panamá, Sobre la Extradición.

Made in the USA
Las Vegas, NV
26 November 2020